THE
FIRST
KOSHARE

Alicia Otis

Sunstone Press
Santa Fe, New Mexico

Dedication

This book is lovingly dedicated
to all dreamers in recovery.

With illustrations by the author.

First Edition

Printed in the United States of America

Library of Congress Cataloging in Publication Data:

Otis, Alicia, 1934-
  The first koshare / by Alicia Otis. -- 1st. ed.
      p.   cm.
   ISBN: 0-86534-144-3 : $8.95
   1. Indians of North America--Religion and mythology--Fiction.
I. Title.
PS3565.T46F5   1990
813'.54--dc20
                                                            90-35788
                                                               CIP

Published in 1990 by SUNSTONE PRESS
              Post Office Box 2321
              Santa Fe, NM 87504-2321 / USA

CONTENTS

''We are such stuff as dreams are made on . . .''
Shakespeare . . . from *The Tempest*

FOREWORD

Dreaming:

  Long ago, myths arose like mists above the Dreaming. From the Dreaming mist, clouds formed and raced across the sky in search of islands where our ancestors — the first dreamers — waited, listened and then felt the legends tapping.

  Modern man, it seems, has grown deaf to tapping. Images, stories and music created by strangers to the mist, flash across our TV and movie screens. Loud noise and static drown the tapping. Inside, we are lost; estranged from self, estranged from our Mother Earth and all the others. Sadly, some of us have come to believe that *inside* doesn't even exist.

  In reality, Dreaming is All That Is. Dreaming is our higher spiritual self empowering, illuminating and giving form in ten thousand different ways to All That Is.

  Dreaming is God, The One, manifest as a universe where a tiny speck of matter called Earth grows creatures who, if they listen carefully with open loving hearts, can hear the voice of God tapping . . . *inside.*

Alicia Otis
Santa Fe, New Mexico 1989

PROLOGUE

BLINK!

Magpie woke up. It was dark and the stars were already out. Skunk was dozing beside the fire. Koshare was digging holes in the dirt. Magpie flew off her bush and landed on Koshare's shoulder.

"Just look at you." Magpie scolded. "Head to toe . . . DIRT! Dirt in your ears, dirt in your mouth . . . soot all over your belly." Magpie twisted around and peered over Koshare's shoulder. "Backside's filthy. How can you go to bed looking like this?" Magpie ruffled her feathers and muttered, "What am I going to do with you?"

"Koshare want stor-r-rry."

"STORY!" Magpie shouted. "A lot of nerve you have asking for a story! What you need is a good pecking and a bath . . . not a story."

Koshare hung his head. His fingers made dirty circles on the white stripe running across his belly.

Skunk raised one eyelid and looked at Magpie, "The older we get the harder it is to remember. . ." he yawned and smacked his lips, ". . .that once, all of us were young and not always very clean." Skunk tried to stand up. CRE-E-E-EAK. The ancient vertebrae rebelled. Skunk froze.

Koshare shivered.

Magpie fluttered to Skunk's side and poked her beak into the bushy white stripe of hair running down his back. Bump, bump, bump. Magpie massaged the ancient vertebrae all the way from Skunk's neck to the root of his magnificent tail.

"Ooooo. . .ah. . .ah," Skunk sighed and then he whispered, "Thanks, Magpie." The old Skunk inched his hind legs underneath his body, balanced his weight on all four paws, and pushed up. Magpie and Koshare held their breath.

"AHHHHH," Skunk smiled and winked at Koshare. "Made it." He took a few wobbly steps toward the fire, stopped, and said, "Didn't somebody here ask for a . . ."

"STORY!" Koshare's face lit up like a jack-o'-lantern. He leapt to his feet, somersaulted over to Skunk, picked him up and placed him on top of a medium sized boulder. Then around and around the campfire Koshare twirled, raising clouds of dust and yelling, "Story time, story time."

Magpie glared at Skunk and snapped, "You spoil him rotten. He's supposed to be clean and sleeping."

"Spoil him?" Skunk sighed and wiped the dust out of his eyes. "Yes, I suppose I do, don't I?" He looked at the stars. Sometimes I get the feeling . . . there's so little time for . . . spoiling our children."

Koshare skidded to a standstill and plopped down in front of the story stone. A log popped and sparks fired into the sky.

"For a few days, Koshare," Skunk murmured, "something brand new has been dreaming inside here." Skunk pointed to his forehead. "Sometimes," Skunk looked straight at Koshare, "brand new dreamings grow out of the oldest legends."

"Koshare dream like Skunk?"

"Don't interrupt," scolded Magpie.

"Every creature dreams." replied Skunk. "This entire world and everything upon it is part of The Great Dreaming. Dreaming is the nature of existence." Skunk shut his eyes. The fire crackled. "I have a feeling, Koshare, that someday you might be a great, great dreamer."

Koshare giggled and chewed the tip of his horn.

"Take that horn out of your mouth," said Magpie. She turned to Skunk and sing-songed, "Sku-u-nk, it's getting la-a-ate."

Skunk chuckled and wrapped his tail around his feet. "Koshare, when the story's over, promise your mother that

8

you'll go straight to bed."

"I promise."

Magpie flew over to Koshare's shoulder and rapped her wing on his nose. "WITHOUT ANY FUSSING."

Koshare nodded, and absentmindedly stuck the horn back in his mouth.

"Koshare-e-e . . ."

"OK, OK." Koshare flipped the horn behind his ear, and lay his head against the story stone. Skunk's voice came from very far away.

"*Before the beginning, everything was dark, silent, whole.* WAY-TAY-SAY . . ."

THE FIRST DREAMING

"Before the beginning, everything was dark, silent, whole.
WAY-TAY-SAY
In the beginning, long before Koshare, first drum thundered, and light
exploded all the darkness. Fire shocked the universe awake, expanding,
burning.
WAY-TAY-SAY . . ."
"Skunk, What's Wa-Way Tt-ta . . .?"
"WAY TAY SAY is living spirit."
"What's S-s-sp-pr . . .?"
"Spirit is the fire of life. You cannot see spirit with your
eyes. Without spirit nothing exists. Way Tay Say is the First
Dreamer who dreamed this story. Sometimes, Way Tay Say
appears in legends as a glowing white coyote."
"OHHHH."
"It's getting la-a-ater," said Magpie tapping her claws.
". . . and later and later," murmured Skunk. He winked at
Koshare and continued with the story.

Long before Koshare, the universe cooled, matter separated and
gravitated. Thus, stars, suns and planets, with their many moons, came
into being.
Before Koshare, wind and rain soothed and smoothed Earth's raspy
skin. This time of cooling toned the mountains. Rivers and arroyos veined
the earth. Rocks and boulders with their private shadows appeared upon
the land. The plains and deserts sprouted grass, flowers and lichens in
colors; purple, orange and yellow. Gentler winds perfumed with juniper
and chamisa hailed bluebirds swooping down the mountain to feed upon
the greening earth.
One spring, before Koshare, when melting snow gushed through arroyo
beds flinging pebbles, sticks, and tumbling tumbleweed . . .

*when Sister Rattlesnake yawned away the last mirage of winter dreams
and shocked herself awake slithering across the ice-cold rocks outside her
cave . . . during this time of greening, earth's belly rumbled and the desert
split. Long Lizard Tail of Wind, streaked down to earth and tossed a seed
into the crack.*

"Excuse me, Skunk . . ." said Magpie. "Do you hear
something . . . unusual?"

Koshare's eyes never left Skunk's face.

"Unusual?" Skunk cocked his head and listened. "Like
what?"

"Sort of like . . . howling. Listen."

Ah-wooooooooo. Ar Ar a-wooooooooo.

"W . . .W . . .AY TAyyy . . . Ssss . . . aaay!" stuttered Koshare.
His eyes were round as saucers.

Skunk and Magpie looked at each other and laughed.

"Koshare, Way Tay Say is a legend-creature, not a real live
howling coyote," chuckled Skunk.

"Ohhhhh."

"Listen," said Magpie, "there it is again."

"Ah-wooooooooo. Ar Ar a-wooooooooo."

"B e-e- u -tee-ful," murmured Koshare.

"Passionate," whispered Magpie.

"Magnificent," extolled Skunk.

They waited and listened but all they heard were hooting
owls and the usual yip, yip, yipping of the neighboring
coyotes. Magpie flew to the top of her lookout boulder, and
scanned the desert.

"Strange sounds at night," murmured Magpie "even if they
are b-b-bea-u-tee-ful, m-make me n-n-nervous."

A grubby finger tapped Skunk's paw. "Story?"

Skunk jumped. The vertebrae crunched. "OW-W-W-W,"

moaned Skunk. Koshare rubbed the lumpy backbone with his finger. After a few minutes Skunk recovered. He smiled and said, "Thanks Koshare. Now, where was I?" Skunk looked around for Magpie. "Magpie," he shouted, "where was I?"

From her station on the lookout boulder Magpie called. *"Long Lizard Tail of Wind streaked down to earth and tossed a seed into the rubble . . ."*

"Thanks." Skunk wrapped his tail around his feet. Nothing moved. *"More turbulence opened Desert's throat and the seed fell in . . ."*

It spun through a tyranny of rocks, slipped between two plates of stone and splashed into a river. Earth's Belly Trout saw the shadow-dot bobbing on the surface of the water. He grabbed the seed, and spat it straight into the Heart of Earth where it ripened for a century of seasons.

One morning during one hundredth spring, the seed, striped black and white, awakened and began to swell. Five days and six nights the seed grew bigger and bigger and B I G G E R.

Sixth day dawned. WAY TAY SAY
The Mountains trembled. WAY TAY SAY
Winds suspended. WAY TAY SAY
Rain ceased falling. WAY TAY SAY
Sun stopped firing. WAY TAY SAY
. . . time strung its arrow, pierced the seed and a full grown Koshare clown, the very First Koshare, exploded through the earth and rose straight up, up, up into the Blue Bowl Sky . . . WAY TAY SAY.

Koshare blushed, clapped his hands over his mouth, giggled, and said, "Story 'bout me."

Skunk smiled. "Looks like maybe you had a beginning after all."

"BEDTIME," Magpie called from her lookout.

Koshare yawned and rubbed his eyes. Without another word he walked into the cave and lay down on his pile of

13

grass. Before the next owl hooted, Koshare was sound
asleep . . . and dreaming."

  WAY TAY SAY.

. . . time strung its arrow, pierced the seed and a full grown Koshare clown, the very First Koshare, exploded through the earth, up, up . . . straight up, into the Blue Bowl Sky . . .

THE FIRST KOSHARE

Raven Passing By, the omnipresent witness of this dreamed and dreaming universe, watches, listens and records all occurences precisely when and how they happen without imposing moral judgments, or relative measurements of time, space or value. RAVEN PASSING BY:

"The New Being touched the sun, arched its back and turned into a rainbow. It spiraled down toward earth. A shadow passed across the sun. The shadow screamed: "KOSH-ARE-E-E-E!" Sparks flew everywhere. Two shadow wings braked the New Being's fall, and shafts of light burst through it's face. Just before it hit the ground I saw an eagle disappear between the New Being's eyes.

"The desert exploded. I circled the impact zone waiting for the dust to settle. The first thing I saw was the New Being's body lying on the ground. Its torso tilted up and leaned back against its arms. Two horns drooped down either side of its huge, round head. The head moved slowly from side to side. I observed the pair of brand new eyes seeing a desert for the very first time.

"It tickled its striped belly and giggled! It discovered its mouth hole and shoved its fingers inside. Wet! What a surprise. It wiggled its toes, touched its nose and nibbled on its horns. Then something, perhaps hunger, made it cry. Fingers touched the tears. Wet! Tears on tongue taste salty.

Its hand scooped up the earth. Desert earth feels dry. Dirt in mouth . . . yuck!

"Touching skin feels good. Chewing horns . . . um-m-m-m, nice. Tongue sticks out of mouth and wiggles like toes. Fingers pick up almost everything.

'What a pleasure it is,' thought Raven Passing By, ''watching a New Being come alive.'

High noon and the desert sizzled. Before Raven Passing By left for cooler places she dropped out of the sky and landed in a bush only a few feet from where Koshare was touching, feeling, smelling and tasting his new home.

"It makes noise that sounds like, "MA-GAA-GOO." Its mouth drools and the fingers smear red desert earth all over itself.

"It tastes everything in sight: pebbles, sticks, grass, mica bits, but when it tasted Grandfather Stink Bug it made an awful face and spat him out."

Raven Passing By blinked her eyes and flapped away.

Zip, zip, zip. Sister Dragonfly whipped through the sky over the desert as fast as she could fly. 'Pretty soon now, pretty soon,' she buzzed. Little Waterhole was her home, not an eternity of rocks and baking sand. Suddenly a gigantic striped "bug" crawling on the desert caught her eye.

"What . . ." murmured Sister Dragonfly, "is that?"

She braked and hovered. Curiosity reversed her flight. Back . . . zip, back . . . zip. She dropped until she hovered right over Koshare's head.

17

"Now that's some bug," whirred Sister Dragonfly. To her surprise the "bug" stopped crawling, pulled its legs underneath its body, and sat up. It's head tilted up and two bright, little eyes stared back at her.

"Goooo. Sluzzzgugg. Ga ga. DA." Its red lips curled up at the corners and its mouth stretched clear across it's face.

"Ga ga ma . . . guzz guzz," gooed the "bug." It tried to touch the dragonfly.

"What an amusing creature," hummed Sister Dragonfly. Her whirring wings glittered in the sun. "You silly bug," she sang. "You can't move off the ground. You can't catch me. Tee hee tee hee." Then she dive-bombed Koshare's head.

"GAAMAA-NANA-GA," Koshare screamed with glee.

"Wonderbug, you sure make a lot of noise," laughed Sister Dragonfly, darting out of reach of the grabbing hands.

"GA-MAA."

One hand nearly caught her, but just in time, Sister Dragonfly shot up into the sky and hovered above Koshare's head. Her wings, sparkled, just barely . . . out of reach.

"DA DA GA-A-A." Koshare crawled after the spinning, glittering wings. Then to the absolute amazement of Sister Dragonfly, "Wonderbug" rolled backwards over its head, stood up and balanced on the feet attached to its bottom pair of legs. It tettered and then fell down. On all fours, it crawled over to a rock and pulled itself up. Again, it balanced, wobbled and fell. When it saw Sister Dragonfly, it tried to totter after her. When it fell it shouted, "GAA . . .Dada Ga GA!" Over and over again, it tried to stand and run after Sister Dragonfly.

"Wonders will never cease," murmured Sister Dragonfly. She hovered a little longer tantalizing Koshare with her gossameer wings and then, zoom, zoom, zoom off she darted straight across the desert, for Little Waterhole.

"Ga?" Wonderbug wobbled after her. "Ga?" It scanned the sky. "Da ga?" Stark blue glared back. Empty space, without a

18

trace of spinning silver wings.

"GA ba-ba." Tears filled Koshare's eyes. Its mouth curved down. "Ga magoo da," it sobbed. Finally it lay down right in the middle of the hot, hot desert and cried itself to sleep.

When Koshare woke up, a pale blue butterfly was standing on its stomach fanning herself.

"GA!" Koshare's big red mouth grinned from ear to ear. "Ka da ma ga" shouted Koshare. It jumped to its feet and grabbed for the butterfly.

"Skss, Skss, Skss," giggled the pale blue butterfly. She fluttered through Koshare's fingers and landed on top of a tall boulder. "Skss, skss," giggled Sister Butterfly, "What a funny looking creature that is . . . skss, skss, skss, skss."

Golden Eagle loved to fly. All day long, he soared around and around the blue bowl sky. Gliding was so restful that he often fell asleep, waking only long enough to look around and change the angle of his feathers. In one such awakening he spied Koshare on the desert chasing the pale, blue butterfly.

"Well, I'll be," murmured Golden Eagle. His eyes were so sharp that from high up in the sky he could distinguish an ant from a flea.

"KOSHARE-E-E-E," Golden Eagle screamed. Like a bolt of lightning he streaked after the butterfly chaser. From the top of the boulder Sister Butterfly opened and closed her wings. She watched and waited.

"KOSHARE-E-E-E-E," the eagle screamed again and zoomed between the New Being's horns.

Koshare fell to the ground and trembled.

"HA HA HA HA HO HO HO HO." Golden Eagle's laughter rippled through the grass. For miles around, every desert mouse trembled and dove for cover. Sister Butterfly fluttered off the rock and vanished out of sight across the desert.

"KOSHARE-E-E-EEEEEE!"

The New Being leapt to its feet and jumped clear over the

boulder where the butterfly had been. When it landed on the other side it scrambled for cover behind a tall rock. It waited and trembled.

In sheer terror Koshare watched Golden Eagle's shadow settle on top of the boulder. Brilliant yellow eyes pierced the shadows and searched behind each stone. "Koshar-r-re?" called the rapacious beak. Yellow eyes looked everywhere until, at last they nailed Koshare hiding behind the tall rock.

Golden Eagle bobbed his head, flapped his wings and repeated the word, "KO-SHAR-Eeee."

"G-G-Ga?" Koshare stuttered. With its eyes glued upon the glowering bird, Koshare slowly backed out from behind the rock.

Again the eagle flapped his wings and repeated the sound, "KO-SHAR-E."

'K-K-KO-SH-sh . . ." stammered Koshare.

The Eagle hopped from one leg to the other and chanted, "KOSHARE, KOSHARE, KOSHARE," over and over again.

Then Golden Eagle and Koshare sang the word together, "KO-SHAR-EE." Only Koshare couldn't make the sound of, "R". He said, "KO-SHA-WEEE."

The eagle fluttered off the boulder and landed beside Koshare sitting on the ground with the smaller stones. "Follow me, follow me," said the yellow eyes that never blinked.

Koshare grinned and stood up. When Golden Eagle danced Koshare danced. When Golden Eagle flapped his wings the New Being flapped its arms. Higher and higher Koshare jumped, danced and flapped. Jump, dance, flap-flap-flap, jump, dance, flap, flap, flap. Suddenly Koshare soared off the ground. Behind the eagle, the New Being flew straight up, up, up into the sky. Just before they reached the sun, Golden Eagle leveled off. He dipped his wings, looked over his shoulder at Koshare and shouted, "KOSHARE-E-E-E-E."

"KO-SHA-WEE-E-E," screamed the black and white horned bird. Koshare soared and glided. "WHEE-E-E-E.

20

WHOOPIE-E-E." All afternoon, Golden Eagle and Koshare flew around and around the blue bowl sky.

The sun turned orange, before Koshare noticed it slipping down, down, down off the edge of sky!

"GA? MA GAA? shouted Koshare pointing its "arm-wing" at the falling sun.

"HA-HA-HA-HA-HA-HAAAAA." The eagle caught an updraft and soared past Koshare up, up, up into the crimson sky.

"AH-H-H-H-H-H," Koshare screamed as he flipped upside down, and tail spinned toward the earth. "AHHHhhhhhhhh." It flapped its arms but nothing happened. When it tried to turn . . . nothing happened. Faster and faster the desert tilted and whirled straight up into Koshare's face.
"AHHHHHHhhhhhh," screamed the big, red, wide open mouth. Before the crash, two shadow wings wrapped around Koshare and broke the speed of the deathly fall, one instant, before the crash.

MAGPIE

Magpie had spent the entire afternoon gossiping with the prairie dogs.
Their squeaky voices talking all at once had left her with a splitting
headache. When the crash occurred Magpie was thinking about two things:
grasshoppers and sleep.

When Magpie regained consciousness, she was laying flat on her back in
the middle of the desert. The tilting, whirling, orange and yellow sky made
her feel sick and so she closed her eyes.

When she woke up the twilight blue was holding steady. Magpie rolled over
on her stomach and panted. When her eyes focused she saw something lying
beside her that she had never seen before; a bare-skinned creature covered with
black and white stripes. It had a huge round head with two ridiculous looking
horns drooping down over its ears. It didn't move or make any noise.

"Just look what you've done?" squawked Magpie. She could
barely stand up. "What are you anyway?" She stared at
Koshare with a look of genuine disgust, "Whatever you are,
you sure messed up my plans for an early supper and a quiet
evening at home."

Suddenly the red lips quivered. The belly jerked and tears
squirted out of its eyes.

"Whatever it is, I guess it's alive." Magpie rolled her eyes
and turned her back on Koshare. She felt dizzy and sick. Her
head sank in between her wings.

"You nearly killed me, you know . . . you . . . you dumbhead."
Magpie's neck feathers twitched as she watched the evening
shadows covering the desert. "Where are your wings? And
your feathers . . . where are they? All I see is bare
striped skin and a huge stupid looking head. A creature constructed like you has no business being up in the air. And
further more," Magpie muttered, "I should be the one who's

crying, not you. I could loose my job over this. I can hardly stand up much less fly." Magpie spread her feet wider apart. "A professional gossip that can't fly," Magpie spun around and screamed at Koshare, "is a DISASTER." Magpie lost her balance and toppled over on her back. She lay sputtering with her feet kicking the air.

Koshare put his hands over his face and sobbed.

"If there's one thing you're good for," squawked Magpie standing up and wobbling close to Koshare's head, "it's CRYING. You're the . . . you're the biggest, ugliest and loudest crybaby I ever saw or heard." Magpie put her wings over her ears and screamed, "STOP THAT!"

Koshare gulped a few times, sat up and stared at Magpie. He swiped at his running nose and rubbed the tears out of his eyes.

"Well, I'll be," exclaimed Magpie, "It stopped! Do you . . . can you . . . understand words?"

"GA," said Koshare. He looked at Magpie and smiled.

"If you understand words, then do you speak . . . words?"

"Ga."

"Ga? What's Ga?"

"Ga."

"Is Ga the only word you know?"

Koshare smiled and pointed to the bump on his head. "OWWWW."

"I see. Well, I suppose Ga and Ow are better than nothing." Magpie scratched her head. "Lets try something else. I'll ask you some questions and . . . and you . . . you just say, ga, or whatever else comes into your mind. Ready?"

"GA."

"What are you?"

Koshare shrugged his shoulders and shook his head.

"You . . . don't know . . . what you are?"

"Ga." Koshare nodded and smiled. Suddenly he made a grab for Magpie's long, glossy tail. She jumped away. "Don't do that," she snapped. "Keep those wiggly paws to yourself."

Koshare looked surprised but he put his hand in his lap.

"Well I'll be," said Magpie. She shook her feathers and said, "You seem to do anything I say, don't you?"

"Ga." Koshare's smile glowed like the moon rising above Red Mountain.

"Where are you from," asked Magpie, "besides up there?" She pointed to the sky.

Koshare shook his head. "Ga."

"Well, I know you're not from here because my gossiping business covers the entire desert between Red Mountain and the Vanishing Hills. And never, in my entire journalistic career, have I come across a creature that looks like you."

Suddenly Magpie was reminded of the precarious nature of her career. "Do you realize," she sputtered, "that this crash may cost me my job. Do you know that there are at least sixty, maybe even a hundred younger magpies out there," Magpie circled her wing around her head, "just waiting for something like this to happen to me."

"Mind you," Magpie jabbed her wing under Koshare's nose, "not one of them has my skill for turning a mundane event into a juicy tidbit of gossip." Magpie hopped on top of Koshare's stomach and flapped her wings over her head, "If I don't recover my balance by tomorrow morning," she shrieked, "I don't know what I'll do .. and ... IT'S ALL YOUR FAULT!" Magpie whacked Koshare on the face with her wing, lost her balance and fell to the ground.

Koshare rubbed his cheek and started to whimper.

Magpie struggled to her feet and glared at Koshare. "Don't you ever stop crying?"

"GA? (sob) . . . Ko-sha (sob)-wee."

"Now what's that suppose to mean . . . Ko-Kosha-wee. I never heard of such a word."

"Ko-sha-wee." Koshare repeated and pointed to himself.

25

"Oh. Then DRAT KO-SHA-WEE!" Magpie squeezed her eyes shut and screamed "SCRABBLEWUZZLEFUZZERWICK!" She spread her feet apart and muttered. "If I had my balance back I'd fly away from here so fast that . . . lightning couldn't strike me."

Koshare blinked his eyes . . . The corners of his mouth drooped and quivered. "Kosha-wee." He pointed to the top of his head and whimpered. "OWWWW."

"Aw, your head hurts, doesn't it?" Magpie cooed sarcastically. "Tsk, Tsk, now isn't that too bad. Look, Ko . . . Ko . . .WHATEVER YOU ARE . . ." Magpie stamped her foot and shouted. "You got me into this mess and I don't feel one bit sorry for you. Anyway, equilibrium or not, I'm leaving."

Magpie flapped her wings, and started to run. But before she gained enough ground speed for a takeoff, she swerved and fell. "See what you've done to me?" screeched the irate bird once more lying flat on her back with her claws stabbing the air. In a few minutes she flipped right side up. Magpie trembled and her eyes glared blacker than the night. Koshare sat quietly staring at the stars.

After Magpie calmed down she hopped over to the New Being and said. "The desert at night is a dangerous place for a magpie who cannot fly. Coyotes, lynx, owls, bobcats, fox . . . every creature that eats magpie hunts after dark."

Koshare smiled. "Ga? Magoo . . . ga?" Ever so slowly, he inched his open palm toward the bird.

Magpie watched the big "paw" moving closer and closer. Her heart was pounding so fast that the white feathers bumped up and down on her chest. "PLEASE, D-DON'T D-DO THAT!" squawked Magpie diving under a bush.

Koshare withdrew his hand, examined the front and back of it, and wiggled the fingers. "Ga da? Ma da?" he thrust his hand under the bush and felt around for Magpie.

"Hey, I told you . . . GET THAT THING AWAY FROM ME."

Magpie skittered out of reach and dove underneath a larger bush.

"GA?" Koshare crawled over to the bush sat down, and waited for Magpie to reappear.

"Look," called Magpie from the bigger bush, "I have to admit, that under the circumstances, I need you for protection. Nothing, not wolves, or even mountain lions would dare come near something that looks like you. But please, I beg you, keep those wiggly paws away from me."

"Ga." Once more the hands neatly folded themselves back into Koshare's lap.

A few minutes later Koshare spotted Magpie's white wing patches emerging from the lower branches of the bush. He leapt into the air, somersaulted and landed on his feet. "Ga, Ga, ga ga ga" he sang with glee, clapped his hands and danced a jig.

"Good gracious," muttered Magpie diving into a thatch of tall grass. She peeked out at Koshare. A jack o'lantern smile brightened his face. He shook his head and the zigzag horns flapped about his ears. He scratched his back and waved his arms. Then he looked up at the sky, flung the wiggly paws over his head and made grabbing motions at the twinkling little lights scattered all over sky.

"GA-A-A-A-A . . . GA-A-A . . ."

"I wonder," murmured Magpie, "if whatever it is, really thinks it can touch the stars?"

"Hey, you . . . " Magpie yelled. "What are you doing?"

Koshare hopped over to Magpie. "GA! MAGOO GA-A-A." Koshare screamed with delight and pointed to the sky.

"Those little lights are stars. You silly creature, you can't touch stars!" said Magpie giggling at Koshare hopping around like a fat grasshopper.

All of a sudden a new sound rang across the desert. "AH-WOOOO AH-WOOOO . . . yip yip yip . . . AH-WO-O-O-O."

"Oh no." Once more, Magpie dove underneath a bush.
"C-Coyotes," she whispered, "Or, or. . .m-m-maybe. . .W-W-
WOLVES. Oh my g-goodness, by-by now, every animal on
this d-d-desert knows exactly where I am."

AH-WOOOO AH-WOOOO. . .yip yip yip. . .AH-WO-O-O-O."

"GA?" With his arms flapping over his head Koshare made
a leap toward the new sound.

"STOP THAT!" screamed Magpie. "Stop jumping and come
over here, sit down and BE QUIET!"

Immediately Koshare somersaulted over to the bush, and
sat down.

"Look, K-Ko-shawee. There are huge, hairy, hungry creatures
with long, sharp teeth out there." Magpie whispered. "They
want to eat m-me but they'll keep away from me if they s-see
you f-first. P-Please s-stay right here b-beside this bush but
keep your p-paws t-to yourself and s-speak s-softly if you
absolutely have to say . . . GA!"

Koshare put his hands in his lap and whispered, "Ga."

T-thanks," mumbled Magpie, "T-thanks Koshawee."

AH-WOOOO AH-WOOOO. . .yip yip yip. . .AH-WO-O-O-O."

The coyotes howled, and Magpie trembled. Crickets sang,
and owls hooted. Like a sentinel, Koshare sat in front of
Magpie's bush staring at the stars. After awhile, the howling
ceased. Magpie crawled into the open and shook the dust out
of her feathers. The pounding in her head was going away. In
spite of the imminent dangers lurking in the shadows,
Magpie's journalistic nose had begun to quiver with the scent
of something utterly *extraordinary*.

STARS

"This Koshawee - whatever it is - maybe the hottest piece of gossip of my entire career," said Magpie watching the New Being sitting with his hands folded in his lap, looking at the stars.

She hopped closer to Koshare and stopped just short of his knees. "You sure like those stars, don't you?"

Koshare looked down at Magpie and smiled. "Ga."

"Stars over the desert are beautiful, aren't they?"

Koshare nodded his head. "Ga."

"Koshawee, do you have any idea where you come from?"

Without a moment's hesitation, Koshare pointed to the sky and said, "Ko-sha-wee." Then he leapt to his feet, flapped his arms like wings and ran around and around in large looping circles. "KO-SHA-WEE-E-E-E," screamed the New Being.

"SH-H-H-H-H-H-H," hissed Magpie. "Get back here, and b-be quiet. My predators . . ." Magpie looking wildly about for any signs of stalking yellow eyes.

Koshare sat down. Once more, his open hand inched toward Magpie. Magpie squeezed her eyes shut. "I'll tolerate anything," she muttered, "to get a story."

"AHHHHHH." Koshare gazed at his finger that touched the silky feathers. "HMMMMM." Once again Koshare reached out and touched Magpie's back. "AHHHHHHH . . ."

"P-P-Please." Magpie shrank back. "Would you s-stop doing that. I . . . I . . . it's just . . ." Her feathers quivered. "You're . . . awfully b-big you know. Horns . . . b-bare skin . . . s-s-stripes . . ." She shook herself and took deep a breath. "I . . . I . . . don't m-mean to be rude . . . but you see . . . I'm f-frightened b-because . . . I never saw anything that l-looks like you."

"Ga? Koshare leaned against a rock and smiled at Magpie.

30

"You're just . . . t-trying to b-be . . . f-friendly, right?"

"Ga," said the smiling, red lips.

Then the striped arm raised above the round head with drooping horns (Magpie shuddered) but this time the stroking finger pointed at the sky. When the face tilted down Magpie noticed underneath the white forehead, a pair of bright, little eyes twinkling in the center of two black triangles.

His finger made jabbing motions toward the sky. The lips moved and out tumbled . . . "'tahs?"

"Oh my gosh," Magpie nearly fell over with surprise. "You said it. STARS!" shouted the utterly astonished bird. "That's right . . . those little lights . . . are called . . . STARS," Magpie laughed. "Hey," she exclaimed, "That's . . . why that's absolutely amazing!"

". . . taahh-z," said Koshare.

"SSS-tar-zzz." Magpie emphasized the "S's". "Put your tongue behind your teeth and blow out. SSSSSSSS-tarsss."

Koshare pulled his lips back and exposed the bluntest, whitest mouthful of teeth that Magpie had ever seen. The jaws opened slightly and out blew a perfect, "SSSSSSSS".

"See," Magpie hopped on Koshare's knee, "you said 'S' perfectly. Now, say . . . SSSSS-T A R -Sss."

"SSSSS-tah-zzzzzz," said Koshare. He looked at Magpie for approval.

"Good! You almost got it right. There's just one sound we missed. Say RRR-rrrrrr." Magpie leaned close to Koshare's face. She opened her beak and the sound. "RRR-rrr" rumbled out of her throat. "R." Magpie explained, "comes from deep inside the throat. Pull your tongue back, and open your mouth and gurgle the air up." Magpie demonstrated, and a magnificent "rrrrrr" rumbled over her tongue.

"Ahhhhh," Koshare repeated. Then he listened.

"RRR," said Magpie.

Koshare nodded his head, and tried again.

"AHHHHH . . . rr . . . AHHH-R! AH . . . RRRRR." Koshare took a deep breath, and with a determined look on his face roared: "RRRRRRR . . . SSSSS -tah-ah . . . ah . . . RRRRRRRrrrr."

BLINK!

It could have been her imagination playing tricks on her, but Magpie swore that every star in the sky blinked the first time Koshare rolled his RRRRRRR's.
"S-sta-RRRRRR!"

"Did you see that?" gasped Magpie. "Everyone one of them . . . blinked."

Koshare jumped to his feet and pointed at the sky. With both arms over his head, he jumped up and down trying to touch the twinkling lights.

"There he goes again." Magpie smiled, "trying to touch the stars." Magpie watched Koshare leap and grab, leap and grab over and over again. "What an extraordinary creature this Kos . . . Kosh . . . Ko . . ." Suddenly, a thought occurred to Magpie. "I'll bet . . . why, of course. Kosha-'wee' is meant to be Kosha-R-e. He just couldn't pronounced the letter R. His name must be . . . KOSHARE."

"OWWWWWWWWWW."

Koshare fell on the ground and rocked back and forth holding his foot in his hands. "OWWWWWWWWW," he cried.

Magpie flew over and landed on Koshare's shoulder. With her wing, she stroke the big round face. "Poor thing, poor thing," she cooed. "You stepped on a sharp stone, and it really hurt, didn't it?"

Koshare nodded and continued to cry.

Magpie fluttered down to Koshare's foot and examined the nicked toe. "The pain will go away in a little while, but in the meantime, please cry softly . . . m-my predators," Magpie peered nervously into the shadows, "have v-very sharp ears."

Koshare clapped his hand over his mouth. When the sobbing subsided into hiccups, Koshare looked at his empty hands. "No s-starrrs," he whimpered.

Magpie tapped Koshare's empty hands with her wings and shook her head. "NO TOUCH," she said. Then she hopped up to his ears and whispered, "only LOOK . . ." Magpie pointed to her own eyes and then brushed Koshare's eyelids with her wings . . . "Koshare only look at STARS."

"OHHHHHHH." Koshare nodded his head. "Look St-arr . . . no . . . t-touch."

Magpie nodded and pointed to herself, "ME . . ." then she touched Koshare, "and YOU . . . LOOK at STARS."

"ME". . .Koshare pointed to Magpie. "YOU". . .He touched himself.

"Well . . . not exactly. You see," said Magpie, "ME' is 'YOU' when You are speaking about yourself." Magpie frowned. "Confusing, isn't it?"

Koshare nodded.

"Watch." Magpie touched Koshare's arm. "Me . . ." Magpie pointed to herself, "MAGPIE. MAG-PIE."

"MAAAG-PIII'".

"Good. Now listen. YOU. . ." Magpie touched Koshare, "YOU ARE. . ?" Magpie held her breath. Her eyes danced. . ."YOU ARE. . ." Magpie jumped up and down and flapped her wings. . ."c'mon,. . ."

"YOU ARE . . ." Koshare stretched his arms over his head and looked up at the stars . . .

"KO-SHA-WE-E-EE-EE," roared the stars.

"Oh!" Magpie gasped.

"NO-O-O-O-O." Koshare shook his fist at all the stars, "I AM. . .," Koshare screamed, ". . .I AM. . .KOSHARRRRE-E-E-E."

KOSHARE filled the wind. All the creatures heard the news.

KOSHAR-R-R-E-E, ruffled through the grass and brushed the sides of rocks.

KOSHAR-R-R-E-E tapped the leaves and plunged down rabbit holes. KOSHARE was a bridge, arching over the night.

WHO AND WHAT

"YIP YIP A-WOO. YIP YIP ARu-u-u-u-uuuu."

"Oh b-boy," stammered Magpie scooting under a bush. "N-now you've d-done it."

"Hoot hoot . . . yip, yip aru-u-u-u-u."

Before long the night sky filled with howling, yipping, hooting, and squeaking creatures.

"WHISH WHISH . . . Wha ish KOSHARE?" whispered the wind.

"WONDER OF WONDERS", blinked the stars.

Magpie peaked out from the deep grass underneath the bush fully expecting to be surrounded by a circle of yellow slanted eyes but instead, she heard a thump followed by, "OWWWWWWWWWW" . . . and then, "WAAA-A-A-A-A-A."

"Not again!" groaned Magpie. She followed the cries until she found Koshare wailing his head off in the middle of a cactus.

"Koshare, get off the cactus and, PULEEZE, STOP MAKING SO MUCH NOISE!"

One arm and one leg at a time Koshare extracted himself. "OWW OWW OW-W-Wwwwww," he cried.

"Aru-u-u-u-uuuu yip yip aru-u-u-u-u." replied the coyotes.

"M-ma-mag-pie . . . OWWWWWWW." Koshare pointed to his buttocks bristling with cactus spines. "Owwwwww," he whimpered suddenly remembering to be quiet.

"Lay down and roll over," snapped Magpie. "I'll pull out as many of these spines as I can before I have to hide. If you absolutely must scream, then put your hand over your mouth."

"Owww . . . owww . . . ow . . . OW!"

"SH-H-H-H-H!"

"Ow ow owww."

"OK, now the other side."

OW OW OW OW WOWW OWOW OW."

Finally Magpie whispered, "You're done." A pile of shiny cactus spines lay scatterd around her feet. Koshare sat up. He wiped the tears out of his eyes and rubbed his sore buttocks.

Magpie grinned. "You know what!"

"Wh- ha-ha-ut?" sniffled Koshare. Magpie giggled, "You're a boy."

"Bo-ho-hoy?" Wh-ha-hat's bo-oy?"

Magpie slammed her wing over her beak to squelch her laughter.

"Wh-hat's bo-y?" Koshare repeated.

Magpie giggled and shook the dust out of her feathers. "Boy is . . . well, lets see . . .," Magpie leaned back on her tail and thought. "Boy is . . ." Then Magpie covered her eyes with her wing and muttered, "that sort of question ought to be answered by a mother . . . not a professional gossip."

For a moment, Koshare stared curiously at Magpie, and then he let the matter drop.

The crickets kept on singing, and the shadows appeared to be completely empty. The coyotes howled but they sounded far away. Nearby a family of mice rustled the tall, dry grass. Magpie sat on top of a bush and basked in the moonlight. Out of the corner of her eye she watched Koshare.

"Koshare," said Magpie fluttering over to the New Being and landing on his shoulder, "Do you realize that in order to survive on earth you must have a fundamental awareness of who and what you are?"

Koshare listened.

"You have a name" said Magpie "and you're a male. Now, the next question is: WHAT are you?"

"W-HUT ARR U?" Koshare grinned mimicking Magpie's voice.

"Don't be smart," Magpie snapped. "Please pay attention to what I am telling you. I am a bird. See, these are my wings . . ." Magpie flapped her wings ". . . and these . . ." Magpie pulled out a feather ". . . are feathers. I am constructed for flying. All Magpies are natural talkers. I have a particular talent for gossip. Therefore, I spend my time doing WHAT I do best: gossiping. Now, you tell me: WHAT ARE YOU?"

"KOSHARRrrrr-EEE."

"No,no. Koshare is your NAME. A name is not who or what you are. Who is a word asking for specific creature definition, and WHAT is a word asking for specific details pertaining to that creature's identity."

Koshare looked confused. He shrugged his shoulders, stood up and turned a somersault. He sat down again, lifted Magpie back onto his knee, scratched his head and grinned. Magpie found herself staring up into the brightest pair of eyes she had ever seen.

"You know something, Señor Koshare?" For some reason, WHO and WHAT Koshare is, doesn't seem nearly as important to me as it did a few minutes ago. I can't imagine what's come over me, but," then to her utter surprise, Magpie threw her wings around Koshare's neck and exclaimed, "I . . . I like you . . . very, very much."

Koshare beamed, and stroked Magpie's back.

"Now listen here . . ." sniffed Magpie after a nice back rub, she tapped her wing on Koshare's nose . . . "there's one thing I know about you that you better take very seriously."

"GA?"

"Koshare is definitely NOT constructed for flying." And then Magpie started to laugh. Koshare joined in and together they laughed and laughed until, Magpie heard the strange voice:

Encounters with New Beings must be taken seriously. How the convergence occurs and the age of the New Being at the time of the meeting determines the nature and the quality of the future relationship.

NEW BEING

Magpie spun around. "Who said that?"

"CHIRRUP CHIRRUP CHIRRUP," sang the crickets never missing a beat. Nothing out of the ordinary sat on top of the bushes, or peered out from behind the rocks. Except for the moon and stars, the sky was empty.

"NEW BEING!" Magpie gasped, "Koshare, is that what you are?"

Koshare made a funny face and shrugged his shoulders.

Magpie felt dizzy all over again. "Koshare stop being silly," shouted the astounded bird. "This is serious business. You heard it didn't you . . . t-that voice s-say-ing: P-*Personal encounters with* N-*New* B-*Beings must be . . . taken . . . s-s-seriously . . .*"

Koshare nodded his head, and absentmindedly scratched his stomach.

"NEW BEING?" Magpie shrieked. She covered her eyes with her wings. "I thought," she gasped peeking through the feathers, "As a matter of fact, I'M ABSOLUTELY POSITIVE," rasped the self-assured voice of the desert gossip, "that New Beings are ghosts or . . . possibly, ancestor spirits, n-not real . . . l-living . . . c-creatures." Magpie ogled the fat Koshare, shook her feathers and announced, "Koshare, tomorrow you and I are going to visit that old skunk who lives on top of Three Rock Hill. He's the legend expert around here. I suppose if anybody knows a New Being when he sees one, it would be him."

While Magpie talked, Koshare discovered that when he poked his fingers in the dry soil, little holes appeared. By the time Magpie stopped talking, Koshare had created a design of finger pokes in the dust. He smiled at Magpie and pointed to his creation. "Stars," he announced beaming with pride.

Magpie stared at the ground, and squinted up at the sky.

"Aw c'mon," she giggled. "You mean, those silly looking paw pokes are supposed to look like stars?"

Koshare nodded. He beamed like a sunflower.

"Well, now," said Magpie looking a little embarrassed when she realized that Koshare was serious about his art, "I suppose a creature of . . . of such unique origins as yourself, sees things somewhat differently than an . . . than an ordinary bird. Which reminds me." Magpie added, "right now, would be a perfect time to explore the specific nature of your, ud . . . rather unusual construction."

Koshare clapped his hands, flipped into a headstand and waggled his feet in the air.

"You don't seem to realize" said Magpie, "but a strange voice coming straight out of thin air, announcing to me that you are a New Being . . . Koshare, that's . . . that's VERY unusual." Magpie hopped over and stood in front of his upside-down face. "If by some fluke of nature, you actually are . . . " Magpie gulped, ". . . A New Being, I suppose you'll need to learn how your body parts work in order to escape your predators."

Koshare flipped right-side-up and then sat down. Magpie hopped up to his knee and scrutinized his form. After a few minutes she announced, "Head to toe, this is how you look: two floppy horns hanging off each side of an oversized head. Mouth has big red lips. The entire body is covered with bare skin decorated with black and white stripes. Walks upright balanced on two short, wide feet bones with five utterly useless claws growing out the end of each foot. The other two legs have wiggly claw-things attached to the end that isn't attached to the body. These claws have some practical use because they can pick things up. The creature walks, runs, jumps and turns over in circles. It likes to stand on its head. It loves to chase stars and . . ." Magpie tickled Koshare on the belly, "it is very FAT!"

Koshare started to giggle and soon both he and Magpie were rolling in the dust, laughing their heads off.

"No offense meant," said Magpie wiping the tears from her eyes, "but I have never seen anything that looks as funny as you. Hey, wait a minute," said Magpie whacking herself on the head, "I wonder . . . Koshare, do you suppose . . . you're constructed to be FUNNY?"

Koshare started to laugh. "Faa-NEE?" he asked, "what faa-nee mean?"

Magpie thought a moment and then she said, "Watch me." Magpie rolled her eyes in different directions, hopped on one foot, and put her tail feathers in her beak. She attempted several unsuccessful somersaults, balanced a pebble on her head and strutted around cackling like a chicken.

Koshare laughed. "Magpie . . . faa-nee?" he asked.

Magpie nodded her head and stopped cackling. "Well, that was the general idea." The pebble slipped to the ground. Suddenly she whirled around. "If anybody sees me acting like this," she gasped, "why . . . I'd die of embarrassment. All magpies, especially the gossips, are serious creatures dedicated to social service. Gossip is very important business, you know. But . . . KOSHARE," Magpie grinned and clapped her wings over her head. "K O S H A R E! Now, there's a creature perfectly constructed to be FUNNY!"

BLINK! . . . Suddenly, a circle of winking eyes surrounded them. Magpie squawked and fluttered to the top of Koshare's head. "K-K-Koshare, h-help. W-we're s-surrounded. L-look . . . just look at all those eyes." Magpie gulped.

"R-round eyes, oval eyes, r-red eyes, b-black eyes and s-s-seventeen p-pairs of b-b-big, hungry, y-yellow eyes." Magpie quivered and held on to one of Koshare's horns. "K-Koshare, t-they're all out there. B-Brother Wolf and S-Sister Fox, c-coyotes, hawks, bats, s-snakes, owls, v-vultures, ravens, bob-cats. . .L-Lynx and all her k-k-kits. And, as if that's not b-bad enough," Mapgie's jaws rattled, "I'll b-bet they all s-saw me. . .acting. . .c-c-crazy. Oh, woe, woe, woe is me. If I s-survive this n-night, by t-tomorrow morning I'll be the l-laughing stock of the entire desert. Oh, woe is me." Magpie dove for the hollow in Koshare's cozy lap and lay there trembling.

Koshare stroked Magpie and stared at all the eyes winking in the shadows.

"Y-you s-silly b-bird," Magpie stuttered. "P-pull y-yourself t-together." She was shaking like an aspen leaf. "I've g-got to s-stop being a f-fraidy c-cat and . . . TH-THINK"

"TH-TH-INK?" said Koshare.

"SHHHHHHHH," hissed Magpie.

"SHHHHHHHH," echoed Koshare.

"STAR-R-RS!" Koshare shouted.

Suddenly Magpie found herself flat on the ground. Her "lap" had turned into a pair of striped legs leaping through the shadows.

"STARS . . . STARS," Koshare screamed with delight, jumping this way and that after the pairs of blinking lights.

Desert stars-eyes flew in all directions: winking, blinking, blinking and winking until, suddenly, every one of them vanished.

Twinkle, twinkle blinked the stars in the sky.

Koshare looked every which way. He peeked under stones, and felt inside the bushes. He ran his fingers between the crevices of rocks. This way, that way, Koshare ran around in circles looking for the lost desert stars.

"Sta-RRs?" Koshare shouted. "Sta-RRs?" He crawled all over the desert. He dug holes like Brother Coyote, and stuck his head inside . . . "Star-rs?", he whimpered. At last, in utter frustration, he sat down and started to cry.

"Koshare," Magpie called from the top of her bush, "You scared them away."

Koshare stood up and ran over to Magpie. "Where Star-r-rs go?" he sobbed.

"Koshare, the lights in the shadows, were not stars. They were EYES. Remember?" Magpie touched her eyes. "Those 'lights' were other creatures' . . . EYES."

"EYY-Y-Y-Y-zzzz?" The grimy hand swiped its runny nose.

"Eyy-zz?" Disappointment passed through Koshare's face.

"Eyes here . . ." Koshare pointed to his own wet eyes and then to the desert. "Eyes there." Then he pointed to the sky. "Stars up there."

"Koshare, living on a planet far, far away from the stars," Magpie smiled a little sadly, "is not all that bad once you get use to it." She flew off the bush, landed on Koshare's shoulder and together they watched the stars fade into dawn.

When the last star left the sky, Koshare sat down on the ground, yawned and rubbed his eyes. "No more stars," he murmured.

"Except for the big, bright star just about to pop over the mountain."

"Oh. OH!" Bright-bright light in blue sky, STAR-R-R?"

Magpie nodded. "It's name is SUN. Sun is closer to earth than any other star in the sky, but even Sun is too far away and much too hot for touching."

Koshare looked at Magpie and started to say something, but changed his mind.

"Everything on earth," continued Magpie, "comes from sun's energy."

Koshare too?"

"Well", said Magpie, "I suppose, like the rest of us, you had to start from somewhere." She yawned and flew over to a bush. "I sure hope that old Skunk on Three Rock Hill can recognize a New Being if he sees one." Magpie stretched her wings. "I don't know about you, Koshare, but I need some sleep. Magpie poked her head outside the bush. "Koshare do New Beings know how to sleep?"

"Sl-sl-eep?"

"SLEEP . . . you know, like this . . ." Magpie climbed on top of the bush where Koshare could see her. She shut her eyes, yawned, locked her claws around the branch and tucked her head underneath her wing.

Following Magpie's example Koshare opened his mouth, breathed in, and looked utterly astonished when a real yawn trembled through his body.

Just before the sun peeked over Red Mountain, Koshare lay down on the ground beside Magpie's bush, closed his eyes, put his arm over his head and started snoring.

Magpie removed her head from underneath her wing long enough to watch the sun rise above Red Mountain. "Mornin' Sun," she called. "As you can see, I'm not going to work today. As a matter of fact, I've encountered something very unusual. He happens to be asleep right beside this bush. I wonder Sun, by any chance . . . do you know who or what Koshare is?"

BLINK!

"A New Being has arrived on Earth. He is The First Koshare. Magpie, you're the First Koshare's mother . . ."

MOTHER

"MAMA!"

Blink!

Magpie opened and shut her eyes. The light was blinding. She moved further inside the bush where it was darker, locked her claws around the branch and dozed. A few minutes passed. "MOTHER!" Magpie screeched, "Now, wait a minute . . ."

"MAMA, MAMA!"

Her perch rattled and Magpie plunged straight up out of the bush into the sky. Flakes of bark rained gently through the branches and scattered on the ground.

"Rattling the roost," sputtered Magpie, hovering over Koshare's head, "is no way to wake a bird. Don't ever do that again!" She dove for Koshare's head. He ducked and somersaulted out of her reach.

Shrieking with laughter, Koshare ran around in circles flapping his arms like wings. "MAMA GO ZOOM," he cried, "MAMA FLY, ZOOM ZOOM ZOOM!"

From the top of her bush Magpie shouted, 'KOSHARE! If you don't stop yelling and sit down right now, I'll . . . I'll bite off your nose."

Koshare stopped running. He shut his mouth, sat down and stared at Magpie. His eyes grew big as saucers.

"Phew," Magpie shook her head. "That's more like it. Now you stay right where you are until I am fully awake and in control of my thoughts."

Magpie took three deep breaths and shook herself. "Some awakening," she muttered. "Mama! It called me MAMA and then it shook me right out of the bush. Tell me, Sun, was I dreaming or awake? I guess I'll never know. But this time, I'm positive that I heard a voice say, 'New Being'. Koshare must be 'one of those', and I'm suppose to be its . . . M O T H E R? Great glorious being." Magpie's head sank in between her wings, "It called me MAMA!"

"GA?"

Magpie straightened up and looked at Koshare standing beside the bush. "GA," said Magpie, "is the word you kept repeating over and over in my dream. 'GA.' But I wasn't dreaming." Magpie squinted her eyes, and turned toward the sun. "Guess what, Sun", she said, "Now I'm wide awake. A very real New Being is standing beside this bush and his name is The First Koshare."

"Sun star too hot. Bright, bright light," whined Koshare covering his eyes with his hands. "Koshare hot."

"Stop whining and go find some shade," grumbled Magpie. She had not finished her conversation with the sun and resented the interruption.

"Mama, what's sh-sha-de . . ?"

"OH . . . SCRABBLEWUZZLEFUZZERWICK!" Magpie screeched so loud that she lost her balance and nearly fell off of the bush.

"Gaaaaa," Koshare cooed. He reached up and steadied Magpie on her perch.

"DON'T TOUCH ME!" snapped Koshare's brand new mother.

Koshare withdrew his hand, and backed away. The red lips quivered and a tear trickled out down his sad, clown face.

Magpie locked her claws around the branch. "Sorry Koshare," she apologized. "I-I know I'm cross. It's not your fault, I suppose, that I'm your MOTHER. Don't take it personally, but I'm just not prepared to be anybody's mother, much less the mother of a New Being that . . . that looks like you. Why, I'll be the laughing stock of this entire desert when all the creatures find out that you are . . . MY SON!" Magpie sat locked on her perch. She opened her beak and panted. The heat was rising.

A short distance from the bush, Koshare stood with his eyes fixed on Magpie. His mouth hung open.

"If you don't shut your mouth, the bugs'll fly in," grumbled Magpie.

Koshare shut his mouth and sat down beside an ant hill. He watched the ants crawling in and out of the little hole leading to their underground maze of interconnecting tunnels.

"How's that for starters, Sun!" sighed Magpie. "Isn't a mother suppose to supervise what goes into her child's mouth? If this Koshare creature were a feathered fledgling, I suppose flying bugs would be the very thing a mother would encourage it to eat." Magpie sighed and closed her eyes. Once more her head sank between her wings.

New beings are spirits that descend upon earth bearing great wisdom. They arrive fully grown, but like children, new beings are unworldly and require parental guidance and protection. They choose their parents. The chosen parent has no choice but to follow the path set forth by the new being's spiritual, physical and emotional requirements.

"Mama?"

Blink! "Yes, Koshare."

"Mamma, look at me!" Koshare waved at his mother from the top of a tall boulder.

"That voice . . . there it was AGAIN!" Magpie sat up looked around. "Where in the . . . ?"

"Mama, look at me," Koshare shouted again. Magpie looked

50

at Koshare and absentimindedly, waved back.

"Voices without bodies . . ." mumbled Magpie shivering ever so slightly, "g-give me the c-creeps."

The desert simmered.

"Da da la la . . . laa, laa, raa, gaa, dada . . .," sang Koshare. He jumped off the boulder and somersaulted around and around Magpie's bush. "Mama, Mama, look at me." He threw dirt in the air, and tried to walk on his hands, but when the first pebble ricocheted off Magpie's head, she shot out straight up into the Blue Bowl Sky and screamed, "LEAVE ME ALONE!" the bush trembled and the desert sizzled.

"Go play somewhere else."

Koshare spun around and there was Magpie sitting on top of another bush.

"Please, Koshare, try to understand. Your . . . your mother needs some time ALONE . . . to . . . to think."

"AH-ALONE?"

"BYE-BYE, Koshare." With her eye on Koshare, Magpie made a wide circle around the desert. This time she wanted to make sure Koshare was safe before she indulged herself in the luxury of solitude.

"Bye-bye, Mama." Koshare skipped over to a patch of sunflowers, and tumbled into a headstand. He picked a sunflower and put it between his teeth. Then he somersaulted over to a huge boulder, leaped into the air, flipped upside down and balanced on one finger on top of the rock.

"What the . . . ?" Magpie hovered over Koshare's head and then landed on ground. "KOSHARE! When . . . did you learn how to do that? I mean . . . good gracious! That's positively ACROBATIC!!!"

With the sunflower flower clamped between this teeth, Koshare somersaulted over to Magpie. He turned around, wiggled his fanny, pirouetted on one toe and pretended to fall down.

"There you go again . . . being funny," giggled Magpie.

"FA-NEE. . .KOSHAR-R-R-E. . .FA-NEE." Koshare leaped into the air, put his thumbs in his ears and waggled his fingers at his mother.

"KOSHAR-R-R-E FUNN-E-E-E-e-e-e." This time, Koshare leap-frogged three boulders in succession and jumped so high that he disappeared inside a cloud passing over the desert.

"Come back here," shouted Magpie.

"Bye-e-e bye-e-e-e . . ." came the sound of Koshare's voice inside the little cloud.

"If you don't come back down here right now," shouted Magpie, "I'll . . . I'll BITE OFF YOUR NOSE."

But the cloud slid beyond the range of Magpie's voice. Turning somer-saults in the air was so much fun that Koshare couldn't resist the temptation and so he jumped off the cloud. When his leap reached the apex of it's arc Koshare somersaulted over and over all the way down to the desert. But, again, he forgot about landing. In the nick of time he spotted a shadow on the side of a steep hill. A perfect landing spot, thought he, and so, with his eyes focused on the darkest corner of the shadow, he crashed and rolled.

"SCRABBLEWUZZLEFUZZERWICK!" screamed the shadow, and to Koshare's horror, a terrible stink filled the air. In spite of an overwhelming attack of choking and gagging Koshare caught a glimpse of a black, furry creature with it's tail sticking straight up in the air. A white stripe ran down the center of its back all the way to the tip of its long, bushy tail.

With both hands clamped over his nose Koshare tore across the top of the hill. Before he reached the edge he tripped over a rock and fell all the way to the bottom. With a resounding THUD he hit the desert and kept on rolling.

SKUNK

Like a crazy wind, Koshare zigzagged a drunken path across the desert. "MA-MA, MA-MA," he cried. "Waaaaa . . . MA-MA . . . MAGPIE-E-E-E . . ." Koshare gaged. His mouth opened and shut. His eyes bulged. He thrashed and kicked, and clouds of dust rolled into the sky.

The smell hit Magpie long before she passed over Three Rock Hill. Obviously something had upset Skunk, the oldest and wisest creature on the desert. This particular skunk also happened to be the legend keeper that Magpie had planned to consult that very afternoon regarding the authenticity of Koshare's mysterious origins.

"I am glad to see that motherhood hasn't robbed me of my gift for sniffing out the news the moment it occurs," said Magpie, trying not to breathe. "First, I'll find out what happened to Skunk and then I'll look for Koshare."

But before Magpie had a chance to learn the news at Three Rock Hill she heard, "MAMA . . . MAMA . . . Magpie-e-e-e . . ." and then she saw the clouds of dust.

"Oh, Oh," Magpie sped over the top of Three Rock Hill, held her breath, and dove into the dust cloud where she found Koshare flopping like a fish on dry land.

"See what you get for disobeying your mother?" screamed Magpie.

"MAMA, MAMA," wailed Koshare. He sat up, and peered

through the swirling debris for his mother.

"Koshare, here I am." Magpie flew back into the dust after grabbing a breath of fresh air. She passed by Koshare's face making sure her wing tips touched his check. "You sure know how to mess things up," Magpie shouted. "I can't imagine how you did it, but you have just crashed into . . ."

At first, New Beings are clumsy. They crash into everything, including deserts, mountain peaks, lakes, trees and other creatures. By the end of the third day most New Beings have successfully completed the initial collisions with their earthly parents.

. . . Skunk." Magpie gulped and flew away from Koshare. The smell of Skunk was overwhelming. "Don't ask any question and follow me," she shouted through the dust. Magpie veered to the left and made a beeline for Little Waterhole.

Koshare ran, stumbled, hopped, and leaped, after Magpie. He followed her to the edge of an arroyo, belly whopped and slid to the bottom. He picked himself up, and with his eyes glued to Magpie's tail, he crashed through dry scrub, tripped over roots and skittered around the spiny branches of jumping cholla. The gully narrowed and abruptly ended in a circle of boulders surrounding a pool of water. By the time Koshare stumbled to the edge of Little Waterhole, Magpie was standing on a rock, waiting for him. "Jump," she shouted.

KERSPLASH! Koshare hit the surface, sank to the bottom, bobbed up and spun around and around. Koshare doused his face and splashed water on his horns. He scrubbed and scrubbed and scrubbed his striped skin until it gleamed.

Magpie giggled and held a wing feather over her nose. "YUCK. You still stink but you're sure the funniest looking waterbug I have ever seen."

"WAA-TER?"

"This is WATER," said Magpie, touching the water with her wing.

"WAA-TER," Koshare splashed the water and watched the shiny substance dribble through his fingers.

"WATER is WET," said Magpie pointing to the liquid dripping off her feathers.

"Wet like sad-eye water?"

"Why yes, Koshare that's right. Another name for 'sad-eye -water' is tears."

"TE-EARS."

Magpie started giggling again. "Koshare, your belly looks like a big striped ball bobbing in the water."

"Koshare b-ball belly . . . b-bobbing water st-stri . . pe?"

Magpie laughed so hard that she nearly fell off the rock.

For the remainder of the morning the weary Magpie rested on the sun-baked rocks surrounding Little Water Hole. Koshare, bouyant as a Halloween apple, splashed around the waterhole and amused himself by grabbing at the curious dragonflies hovering over his head.

"Who is this giant waterbug?" buzzed the dragonflies amongst themselves. "What, what, what is it?" they sang as they zipped forward and backward between Koshare's horns. "Where is it from?" they asked the sun that was making violet and emerald sparkles on their wings.

When Magpie woke up from her nap, she yelled to Koshare." You stay right here and soak yourself. I have to go to Three Rock Hill and speak to Skunk, alone."

Koshare made a bad face and whined. "SKUNK STINK. SKUNK BAD CREATURE. KOSHARE NO LIKE SKUNK."

"You'll feel better when the stink wears off," Magpie replied. She stretched her wings in preparation for the flight.

"Skunk bad, bad, awful stink creature," persisted the monolithic striped bug floating in the middle of Little

Waterhole.

"Be a good creature," called Magpie as she took off over the water. Over her shoulder she shouted, "AND, MIND YOUR MOTHER." She blew Koshare a kiss and soared up, up, up over the top of the arroyo. "BYE-BYE." Magpie's voice streamed back from the empty sky and bounced up and down on the rim of the arroyo. "BYE-BYE-E-E-Eeeee."

Three Rock Hill, resembled a gnarled tree stump, jutting straight up in the middle of a wide, dry plain. Tufts of dry yellowish-brown grass blew stiffly in the wind. Skunk, the ancient hermit resident of this rocky edifice, was the sage, the arbitrator and legend keeper of the desert. At one time or another, every creature living on the desert had made at least one pilgrimage to Three Rock Hill. Besides telling legends, Skunk mediated disputes between the birds and the great families of wolf, coyote, fox, cat, and prairie dog. Skunk offered advise and compassion to the jilted and bereaved. One session alone with Skunk usually straightened out a rebellious fledgling or pup. Skunk's ability to make peace between the headstrong sun and the haughty spirits of thunder and lightning had more than once, saved the entire desert civilization from dying of thirst.

Occasionally, Skunk announced a public story telling. For one week, the creatures of the desert gathered at Three Rock Hill and listened to Skunk, re-tell the many legends of the Vanishing Hills; from the First Dreaming, all the way to 'modern times' During these gatherings, all personal disputes between creatures were suspended. The hunters and the hunted sat side by side listening to Skunk recreate the legends of Way Tay Say, Lo Ka Ree, and Ki Sa Loo. The few remaining survivors of Skunk's genera-tion said that in his prime, Skunk could 'talk story' for two whole days and nights without stopping.

But recently, due to the discomfort of advanced arthritis, Skunk asked Raven Passing By to make it known all across the desert that he wished to spend the rest of his days in silent meditation, alone, on Three Rock Hill. Therefore, all the creatures were aware that only under rare

57

circumstances was anyone welcome at Three Rock Hill.

"Hello-o-o Sku-u-u-unk," called Magpie. "It's Magpie. I used to be the desert gossip . . . remember me?" Magpie circled around and around the top of Skunk's cave. "Skunk, I need your advice. Something very unusual has happened upon this desert. Please, come out and talk to me." An impenetrable curtain of silence, rank with "Eau de Skunk", suspended over Three Rock Hill.

"Sku-u-unk," yelled Magpie, "Please excuse the intrusion on your privacy, but I have something important to tell you. I promise I won't stay long."

Stones glared and the boulders hissed. The smell of Skunk was ominous. The silence shouted, "GO AWAY!"

"Skunk . . . I'm waiting. It's hot up here, and my wings are killing me. Please, may I land?"

After more silence, Skunk's erect tail emerged from the cave. Very slowly the rest of him followed. He squinted up at Magpie and with a short downward thrust of his nose, he motioned her to land.

Magpie settled on a boulder upwind of Skunk. "Thank you for letting me land," she said. "H-How are you feeling?"

"Rotten, thank you. As a matter of fact, I have never felt worse." Skunk took a few wobbly steps, and then stood still.

"Sorry about that," said Magpie, diving for a shadow and fanning herself. "Arthritis bothering you again?"

"Arthritis . . . " growled Skunk, "Ha! That's nothing. This morning a huge striped monster fell out of the sky and landed right on top of me."

"Wow," Magpie shook her head, "I'll bet that hurt." Her wings quivered with compassion.

"Not one part of my body escaped the incredible tonnage of that . . . that . . . monster!" Skunk's voice crackled with rage but the look in his eyes revealed that incredible pain wrought havoc throughout his entire body.

"Señor Skunk, I am very sorry this accident occured . . . As a matter of fact, I too, have recently recovered from a similar encounter with this . . . ah . . . monster." Magpie took a deep breath and forged ahead. "I have some reason to suspect . . . that the monster is actually a New Being. His name is Koshare, and that is why . . ."

"What do you know about New Beings?" snapped Skunk. "The only thing magpies know about is gossip! And gossiping," muttered Skunk, "is an utter waste of time, especially mine." Skunk started to back inside his cave.

"Skunk, wait," pleaded Magpie. "I need your advice. Please allow me to bring Koshare up here so you can tell me if . . ."

"NO!" roared Skunk.

". . . HE IS, OR IS NOT A NEW BEING."

"NO, NO, NO!"

"HIS NAME IS KOSHARE!"

"Listen, nosy bird," Skunk roared. "Never, under any circumstances, will that monster ever be welcome on Three Rock Hill." Skunk disappeared inside the cave. "Gossipmonger," rumbled the voice of Skunk inside the darkness, "if you promise to leave here the minute I'm done talking, I'll tell you all you'll ever need to know about New Beings."

"I PROMISE," rasped the thoroughly insulted bird.

"Rarely," rumbled the barely audible voice, "if ever, do New Beings appear on earth. They're imaginary creatures, existing only in stories and legends. In the days of our ancestors, New Beings fell out of the sky, fully grown and completely innocent. New Beings are the most extraordinary dreamings of Way Tay Say. Good day."

"Thank you, Skunk, for the information about New Beings." Magpie paused, hoping for at least a kindly good-by from the ancient legend keeper of the desert, but not another sound came out of the cave. Once again, gathering all her courage Mapie shouted inside the cave, "Several days ago, the same creature fell out of the sky and crashed into me. Believe me, Skunk, strange things have been happening ever since. You just told me, New Beings drop out of the sky. What am I to make of this phenomenon?"

"You have some nerve, you dingbat bird," bellowed the voice from the cave," telling me that striped devil monster is . . . is a New Being. RUBBISH! Your gossip mind is filled with nothing but LIES & RUBBISH. NOW WITHOUT FURTHER ADO, DO ME A FAVOR AND LEAVE THIS HILL AT ONCE!"

"As far as peace talks go," muttered Magpie making one last circle over Three Rock Hill, "this one leaves a lot to be desired."

She banked her wings and headed for Little Waterhole.

RED MUD MONSTER

Koshare spotted Magpie the minute she appeared over the top of the arroyo. "MAMA, MAMA, LOOK AT ME," he shouted.

Magpie looked down, and what she saw nearly caused her to crash into one of the tall rocks surrounding Little Waterhole. A ghoulish, grinning, mudhead attached to a fat body waved at her from the middle of a pit of thick red mud. Not a drop of water remained in the waterhole. The Red Mud Monster kicked its legs and screamed, "MAMA, MAMA, look at me!"

Mud was splattered all over the rocks and bushes. Tilting mud castles lined the rim of the Little Waterhole. One by one they slid back into the pit and splattered all over Koshare. The Red Mud Monster tossed a handful of mud in the air. KERSPLAT! It landed on the rock beside Magpie. She dodged but a large glob slapped her on the side of her head. Another hit her chest. Exploded mud oozed down the rock and dribbled onto the grass.

Koshare giggled, kicked his legs and rolled over on his belly. "Momma, look. Koshare playing."

The sucking mud went, SCRITCH, SCRITCH, SCRITCH.

"Get out of there!" screamed Magpie. She flew off the rock, and landed on Koshare's shoulder. She clamped her claws into his neck and rivited her beak up and down each side of the big, round, extremely ugly head.

"OW-W-W-W OW-W-W-W," howled the Red Mud Monster. He tried to climb out of the pit but the edge was too high and much too slippery to secure a handhold. Each time he tried to escape, he slid back inside.

"Perhaps. . .PECK PECK PECK. . .Skunk was right. . .PECK PECK PECK after all," hissed Magpie, "Right now . . . PECK PECK PECK . . . you look just like . . . PECK PECK PECK . . . a

61

monster."

"OW-W-W WOW-W-W," Koshare screamed. "OW-W-W-W-W."

With Magpie clinging to his neck, Koshare tumbled, rolled, slipped and slid all around that slimy, waterless pit. A dragon scream bellowed out of the cracked red mouth, and the monster, desperate to escape the relentless beak of Magpie, finally lurched up and over the edge of that hellish pit of mud.

"Wh-why (OWWW) . . . M-Mama(OWWW) . . . bite Koshare?" sobbed the Red Mud Monster thrashing on the grass.

"I'll tell you why when you climb up on the rocks and SIT DOWN!" For safe measure Magpie grabbed Koshare's earlobe in her beak and gave it a good tweak. Koshare scrambled to his feet and in two leaps he was standing on top of the tallest boulder surrounding the empty water hole.

"SIT!" Magpie gave the ear lobe a final twist, and then let go.

"OW-W-W-W-W-W" howled Koshare rubbing his bleeding ear. "OW-W-W W-O-W-W-W-W." With his other hand he massaged the welts raising all over his neck and on the top of his head.

"Best remedy I know for pecking bumps." cackled Magpie with a witch-like grin, "is mud."

Koshare stuck out his lower lip and whimpered, "Mamma, not funny."

Magpie turned her wings into a broom and swept the drying mud off Koshare's leg. Then she hopped up on the tidied spot of bare skin, and slammed her wings on her hips. "Now listen to me. We have to have a serious talk." Magpie looked worried and cross. "Water is scarce. In a hot, dry desert, water is more precious than . . . stars! Without water to drink, creatures die. Koshare, don't you ever . . . EVER, EVER," Magpie rapped Koshare across his nose with her wing, "throw water out of any waterhole ever again."

Koshare stared down at the ugly pit of mud. He picked up a wet glob clinging to the rock and dumped it on top of his head. Mud oozed over his eyebrows and slid over his ears. In spite of herself, Magpie had to laugh.

"Red Mud Monster, now do you understand why I was angry?"

Koshare nodded his head and stared at his feet. He wiggled his toes and watched the thin layer of drying mud crack into a thousand tiny zig-zag lines. "Skunk bad monster, NOT Koshare," mumbled the New Being.

"Whatever made you say a thing like that?" said Magpie. "I only called you that for fun. Just because you look like a monster, doesn't mean you really are one." Magpie thought a moment and then it dawned on her, "Hey, what do you know about monsters?"

"Awful-Skunk-Stink-Creature scream at me: 'MONSTER, GO AWAY!'"

"Yeah . . . well. I suppose he did, didn't he." Magpie ducked her head underneath her wing to think. After a minute she emerged and said, "Koshare, Skunk didn't really mean that you were a real monster. Try to understand that Skunk had never seen anything that looked like you until this morning. Suddenly, there you were dropping out of the sky, feet first heading straight for him. You're very big, you know, and awfully fat. Besides, you don't look anything like other creatures on this desert. When you crash-landed, Skunk's little body was crushed beneath you. You're very heavy, you know, and Skunk is old . . . his bones are fragile. Skunk was terrified and in a lot of pain. Can't you see why Skunk thought you were a monster?"

Absent-mindedly Koshare nodded his head. He scratched, and scratched and scratched himself all over.

"Itching, huh? Dry mud on the skin makes all creatures itch. Follow me."

Magpie led Koshare out of the arroyo and back up to the desert. She showed him how to roll and scratch his skin in the sand. Soon the mud had disappeared and once more, Koshare sparkled black and white.

The sun was setting. Magpie located a tall, leafy cottonwood for roosting and then she flew off to hunt for grasshoppers. Koshare walked off by himself to forage.

At twilight, when Magpie had finished eating, she returned to the cottonwood. She found Koshare seated underneath the tree with his head leaning against the trunk. His mouth was wide open and he was snoring. His hands were locked around his swollen belly. Piled all around him were bits and pieces of spat out leaves, bark, nutshells and chewed up roots too tough to swallow.

"It's a good thing you came here knowing how to forage," Magpie said to the sound asleep Koshare. "If I had to rustle up enough food to fill that big belly, why, why I'd be way too pooped to gossip much less stalk the laziest grasshopper alive.

Before nightfall, Magpie taught Koshare how to pull grass and pat it into a bed. Koshare spread the grass around the base of Magpie's cottonwood and before the stars came out, they both were snoring.

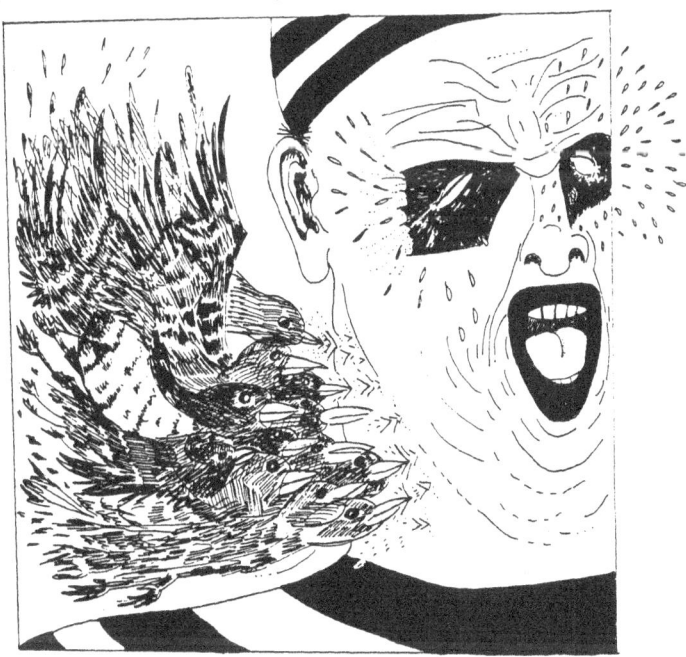

SURPRISE

"Hey yea YEA, hea yea yea YAH, hey hey yah . . ."

"Mmmm. Feels go-o-od," murmured Magpie.

"Hay hay yea . . ." Koshare sang and stroked Magpie's back.

BLINK!

"KOSHARE! What are you doing way up here?"

". . . hey, yea, yea YEA . .." Koshare smiled. His blunt, white teeth flashed in the sunlight.

"I have to admit, in just one day, your waking technique has certainly improved." Magpie yawned and stretched her wings.

Koshare beamed.

"How did you manage to climb to the top of this tree from way down there?" Magpie and Koshare peered down, down, down through the tangle of leaves and branches to where Koshare's grassy bed lay scattered on the ground.

"Look at me." Koshare grinned. He grabbed the limb above his head, and swung hand over hand down through the tree until he reached the bottom branch. He somersaulted to the ground, grabbed a handful of leaves and stuffed them into his mouth.

Then Koshare jumped and grabbed the lower limb. He swung up through the branches and plopped down beside Magpie swinging his feet and chewing leaves. A stream of green leaf juice dribbled down his chin.

"Wipe your mouth," said Magpie loosening her grip on the branch and hopping onto Koshare's knee. Koshare licked his lips, grinned at Magpie and put his finger under her chest. Without any hesitation she climbed aboard and hitchhiked up to his shoulder.

"Whee," chirruped Magpie. "This is fun."

"Dum dee dum, riddley dee." Koshare leaned over and

planted a juicy, green kiss on the top of Magpie's head.

"What the . . .?" sputtered Magpie jerking her head away from Koshare's mouth. The sopping kiss ran down Magpie's face and stained the feathers green, green, green on her snow white chest. When she shook her head globs of half-chewed leaf flew every which way, catching on the branches and sticking to Koshare's chin.

"What's THAT suppose to mean?" sputtered Magpie staring at the green stains on her chest.

"KISS," Koshare looked adoringly at his mother.

"Kiss? What's . . . KISS?"

Koshare pursed his lips, leaned over and . . .

Magpie ducked, flew to another branch and said, "OK, OK, Kiss means . . .?

"Love!"

"Oh, LOVE? Koshare, what do you know about love?"

Koshare's face glowed.

BLINK!

New Beings are the most extraordinary dreamings of Way Tay Say.

Magpie gasped, "That voice again repeating Skunk's exact words . . ." Her tail feathers flashed purple and green. Magpie's claws locked around the branch and she sat very still waiting for her thoughts to settle. Then she hopped onto Koshare's shoulder.

"Kiss. That was nice. A little wet and green but nice. Thanks, Koshare. Now, guess what! After we finish eating breakfast, I have a SURPRISE."

"Sss-SR-rrr . . . PRr . . . RIZzz?"

"SUR-PRISE looks like this." Magpie clapped her wings together, jumped up and down, widened her eyes, opened her beak and exhaled, "OHHHHHhhhhh."

"AHHHH." Koshare's eyes glittered. He clapped his hands and shouted, "Koshare want surprizze NOW!"

"No," said Magpie holding her ground. "Eat first . . . and then surprise."

"Surr-prizz NOW!"

"Koshare-e-e-e, remember this?" said Magpie tweaking his ear.

"Owwwwwww." Koshare jerked his head away from Magpie and covered his ear. He kicked the branch hanging under his feet. "OWWWWW.WW" Real tears burst out the corners of his eyes as he grunted over his fat stomach in an attempt to touch his bruised toes.

Magpie flew out of the tree. "When I return from my breakfast flight," she shouted over her shoulder, "I expect to see you sitting on the ground under this tree finishing up your morning meal."

Magpie circled the cottonwood and headed for the open desert. She spotted some tall grass blowing in the wind, landed and waited.

"Come, come, Grandfather Grasshopper," Magpie crooned. "Let me watch you leap. How I admire your choice of flexible landing spots, such as stems of grass perfectly designed for holding your wee body. When Koshare leaps, he lands in places too hard, like earth, or too soft . . . like Skunk and me."

A grasshopper jumped, and made a three point landing on a blade of grass. Up and down it bounced right in front of Magpie's face.

"Grandfather Grasshopper," sighed Magpie, moving her head in time to the bobbing blade of grass, "Today, I learn from the grass the art of bearing heavy loads because . . ." in a lightning movement Magpie snatched the grasshopper . . ." becauzz, itch up chu me," she hissed between clenched jaws, "chu introduch Koshawee chu hizz fazzer."

69

With mounting concern for the Herculean task ahead of her, Magpie, statuesque and silent, waited for her second course.

After gobbling up three ladybugs and two more grasshoppers she returned to the cottonwood. Koshare was leaning against the trunk surrounded by empty piñon shells, and half-chewed, spat out globs of leaf apparently too tough to swallow.

"I see you've been eating," said Magpie landing on Koshare's shoulder. "You better be full, because I foresee a long walk in your immediate future." With a twinkle in her eye she sidled up to Koshare's ear and hissed, "S-S-S-S-surr . . ?"

"SURPRIZZZZzzzz!"

An instant before Koshare leaped into the sky Magpie departed her unreliable shoulder perch exchanging it for a lower branch of the peaceful old, cottonwood. Koshare turned three perfectly executed airborne somersaults and landed upright on the branch next to Magpie.

"Are you ready for the surprise?"

Koshare jumped up and down on the branch, catapulated out of the tree down to the ground, and back onto the rocking branch. "READY!" he shouted.

Magpie squeezed her eyes shut and locked her claws around the branch . . . "The surprise is . . ." she took a deep breath. "This surprise is" she repeated, ". . . this morning I'm taking you to Three Rock Hill to introduce you to Skunk."

Koshare's face collapsed like a pricked balloon. He sat down with a thud. The branch hit the ground and snapped back into place.

"NO! NO! NO!" Koshare kicked his feet, and wailed, "SKUNK STINK BAD CREATURE. MAMMA TELL KOSHARE AWFUL SUR-PRIZZE." Koshare started to cry all over again.

"Koshare," said Magpie, "You are acting like a spoiled brat. Stop wailing and listen to me."

Koshare shut his mouth. He wiped his eyes, hiccupped and stared at his swinging feet barely missing the punishing branch. When the tree stopped rocking Magpie continued.

"Skunk only smells when he is frightened. Most of the time, like today, for example, Skunk smells just like us. Sniff yourself, Koshare. Smell me, sniff anything you see around here, and you'll discover the natural smell of Skunk."

Koshare put his arm up to his nose. SNIFF SNIFF SNIFF. He smelled his horns, legs, hands and feet. He sniffed Magpie up and down her back and underneath her wings. He smelled her beak and claws.

"OK." Koshare nodded his head. "Koshare and Mama smell OK. But why Skunk smell OK now?"

"Why?" Magpie huffed her feathers. "Koshare, I've told you before, don't ask "why" anything. Why's make lies. Start your questions with who or what. Now, in response to your question, today, Skunk isn't angry or frightened. That's the reason he doesn't stink." Magpie unlocked her claws and hopped onto Koshare's knee. She looked him straight in the eye and in an uncompromising tone of voice she said. "Koshare, I promise. Today, Skunk smells normal. To promise something means to swear in the light of Way Tay Say that the truth is being spoken."

Koshare leaned his head against the trunk of the cottonwood, and stared at his feet. "What's . . . Wa-Way -T-ta . ..?"

"Now that's a perfect question for you to ask Skunk after you get to know him a little better. Which reminds me," chiurruped Magpie, "I forgot to tell you something else. Skunk is the Legend Keeper of this desert. He tells stories better than any creature in the whole world. Skunk knows many, many stories about Way Tay Say."

"Oh." Suddenly Koshare looked down and smiled at

Magpie. "Skunk know story 'bout STARS?'"

Suddenly Magpie's throat constricted. "Why, ah, of course. As a matter of fact, Skunk knows lots of stories 'bout stars.'"

"Hooray," said Koshare clapping his hands, "Let's go!" He somersaulted off the branch and landed on the ground.

Magpie's belly flip-flopped. "T-Three Rock Hill", she shrilled, "is a long walk from here. We ought to leave right away to make sure we get there before Skunk takes his nap." Magpie fluttered off the branch of the kindly, old cottonwood and flew up into the stark, utterly empty, blue, blue sky. She circled once around the tree and shouted, "Koshare, stay behind me at all times. Don't you dare walk, leap, jump or somersault in front of me. We must approach Three Rock Hill very carefully and quietly. Skunk hates surprises. S-surprises, make S-Skunk s-stink."

All morning long Koshare followed Magpie across the desert. Not once did he forget her warning. Sometimes he somersaulted backwards. Sometimes he twirled around in circles. Every now and then he chased a dragonfly, but only sideways. Several times, when Magpie swooped down to check on Koshare she heard him singing;
'Hey yea, I play with Skunk.
Today, hey, yea, I play with Skunk.'

Within her vast, all encompassing shadow Raven-Passing-By spied Magpie and Koshare walking across the desert toward Three Rock Hill. She thought to herself. 'What motivates this odd pair of travelers to accompany each other on a pilgrimage to Three Rock Hill? Could it be that Skunk is feeling better and talking story once again?'

As Magpie and Koshare drew closer to Three Rock Hill, Magpie's anxiety mounted. With increasing frequency she shuttled back and forth, between her elevated sky view of Three Rock Hill and the lower elevation of Koshare's shoulder. Nervousness caused Magpie to jabber even more than normal.

"Remember Koshare, Skunk's memory of you is frightful. He truly believes that you are a monster."

"I'm tired."

"Koshare, you must be sure to make Skunk laugh so that he sees you as you truly are, a funny creature and a promising acrobat. Koshare, if you make Skunk laugh, he'll adore you, I promise."

"I'm hot."

"OK, OK! So am I. What do you want me to do turn off the sun?"

"Momma, my feet hurt, why?"

"For the same reason that my wings ache. Stop complaining."

"Why aren't we there yet?"

"Because Three Rock Hill is farther away than you want it to be, that's WHY. Pretend that Three Rock Hill is farther away than the stars then, before you know it, we'll be there."

"Why?"

"KOSHARE! YOU'RE DRIVING ME NUTS. Why this. Why that. Why EVERYTHING! What have I told you a thousand times already about WHY? Now it's my turn to ask you a question. WHAT makes Three Rock Hill seem so far away?"

"Because I'm tired and my feet hurt."

"See? You answered your own question. Being tired is a fact. Being too hot is also a fact. You have tender feet because you have never walked this far on a hot, dry desert. Walking is a slow, but safe means of getting from one place to another. Yesterday, I'm not sure how you got to Three Rock Hill, but surely, it wasn't on foot. Now, do you have any more questons before we resume our journey?"

"Yes, What make Skunk stink?"

"Now, there's a well phrased question. All skunks have a scent gland, inside their body, located near the base of their tail. This gland holds the ghastly smelling liquid with which you are only too familiar. When frightened or angry, skunks squirt the smelly substance out of their bodies to protect them from their predators. Stink is Skunk's only means of self-preservation in a desert teeming with drooling, hungry, howling creatures.

"Ohhhh." Koshare nodded his head and then he asked, "What Skunk eat?"

"Skunk eats insects, eggs, plants, mice and . . . birds."

"BIRDS??" Koshare blinked his eyes, and pointed at Magpie. "Mama bir-r-r . . . "

"Koshare, don't worry. This particular skunk wouldn't think of eating me because . . . " Magpie smiled and coyly pruned a feather, ". . . because I'm S-skunks f-friend." Pitapat pitapat pitapat fluttered the fibbing little heart.

You have some nerve, you dingbat bird, standing there and telling me that striped devil monster is . . . a New Being. RUBBISH! Your gossip-monger mind is filled with nothing but TRASH & RUBBISH. GOOD-BYE!"

"Help," whimpered the frightened bird quaking inside her flamboyant quills flashing purple in the brazen sunlight. "T-there's that v-voice r-repeating S-Skunks exact w-words. D-Do you s-suppose it knows the t-terrible truth? The fact that Skunk never wants to see Koshare or me, on Three Rock Hill . . . ever again? Oh woe is me, woe is me."

Suddenly looking fresh as a daisy, Koshare back flipped into the sky. "Momma," he shouted over his shoulder. "What means, 'woe is me'?"

"N-never mind, Koshare. I'm just a little hot and t-tired. Lets go." Magpie took off and banked in the direction of Three Rock Hill. "Mamma?" shouted Koshare at the black dot disappearing inside the searing pot of blue, "You think Skunk know story . . . 'bout me?"

New Beings rarely, if ever, actually appear on earth. They are imaginary creatures, existing only in stories and legends!

Pita pat, pita pat pata pat . . .

BOO!

Just as he reached the crest of a long sloping hill Koshare stumbled and fell. "MAMA," he wailed, "I can't move."

Magpie dropped out of the sky and landed on top of Koshare's stomach.

"Koshare, look." Magpie pointed to the perpendicular burl of sandstone and boulders rising directly from the heart of a sweeping span of desert, "That's Three Rock Hill."

"I don't care. I'm hot," whined Koshare. "I don't like it here."

"Stop complaining, and pull yourself together," snapped Magpie, "we'll be there before you know it."

Koshare sat up, and pulled off his moccasins. Magpie hopped up to his shoulder.

"Owww-wow," he moaned softly under his breath. "Owwwwwww." Koshare rubbed his swollen feet and when one of the zigzag horns sagged down into the middle of his face he slapped the bothersome thing out of the way. Unfortunately, the momentum of this blow caught Magpie off guard and sent her spinning, head over tail feathers straight up into the Blue Bowl Sky.

"What do you think, you're doing?" squawked the reluctant acrobat, scrambling to her feet and shaking the dust out of her feathers. Before Koshare had time to think of an appropriate response a flash of pain shot through his tender flap of ear.

"OWWWWWW!" Real tears shot out of Koshare's eyes.

"Nexcht time, you big oaf . . . look before you schwing, "Magpie hissed between clenched jaws. She gave the ear lobe a final twist and made a beeline for the far end of Koshare's shoulder where premeditated escape was a possibility should the necessity arise.

Koshare stuck out his lower lip and rubbed his ear. He dug his toes underneath the dry, crusty surface of the desert.

"Mama bad creature," he whimpered under his breath. The powdery dust soothed his blistered feet.

Magpie stared at Three Rock Hill. Her head was pounding. After a few minutes she shook herself, hopped toward Koshare's ear and bellowed. "WHEN WE GET TO THREE ROCK HILL . . . "

"MAMA!" Koshare frowned and pulled his head away.

Magpie followed the ear, ". . . YOU STAY BELOW. I'LL GREET SKUNK, ON TOP, ALONE . . ."

Koshare clapped his hands over both ears.

". . .AND PREPARE HIM FOR YOUR VISIT. . .TAKE THOSE HANDS OFF YOUR EARS AND LISTEN TO ME!" screamed Magpie.

"STOP SCREAMING," shrieked Koshare staring Magpie straight in the eye.

"I AM NOT SCREAMING!" Magpie looked surprised, and then embarrassed. "I am screaming aren't I. S-Sorry. I'm j-just . . . a l-little n-nervous."

"NER-VUS?"

"N-n-ever m-mind. . ." Magpie trembled, "J-just k-keep c-calm."

Pita pat pita pat pita pat.

She moved away from Koshare's ear, took a deep breath, and started squawking in her usual raucous voice. "When I tell you to leave your hiding place come out in the open. Stand on your head, wiggle your ears, twirl on your toes, make funny faces . . . do anything that will make Skunk laugh."

Koshare sighed, hung his head between his knees and looked bored.

"K-Koshare, just one more thing. DON'T COME TO THE TOP OF THREE ROCK HILL UNLESS SKUNK INVITES YOU."

"Why?"

"WHY!!!!?"

"OK. OK. What. . . ? Who. . . ?" Koshare paused and contemplated his question. Then he slapped himself on the forehead. "Oh oh. . ." He looked at Magpie and then stared blankly up at the stark blue sky. "Question go, bye-bye."

"AHA!" grinned Magpie. "A question forgotten, is a question better not asked, and now . . . lets get moving." Magpie took off and turned toward Three Rock Hill wishing she felt as brave as she sounded. "Sun," she muttered, blinking her eyes at the fiendish ball of fire, "wish me luck."

Waves of heat enveloped the bird in flight. Up and down, down and up Magpie bounced across the blue. The desert sizzled all the way to Three Rock Hill.

They made a wide circle around Three Rock Hill approaching it from the eastern side, where Skunk couldn't see them. When they came to a pile of rocks and boulders at the bottom of the hill, Magpie hid Koshare in a shadow between two large boulders. Then she flew up to the top and found Skunk still deep in meditation seated on top of his Thinking Stone.

"Phew. We made it," Magpie dropped down and hovered over the ancient legend keeper. "Way Tay Say," she prayed, "HELP!" One thousand butterflies fluttered inside Magpie's belly.

Pita pat pita pat, pita pat.

"HALLO-O-O . . . SKU-U-U-UNK."

Silence.

"Are you feeling better today?" Magpie circled around and around the Thinking Stone.

SILENCE.

"Sku-u-unk . . . I brought someone with me who will make you feel w-wonder-f-ful."

Skunk craned his neck, spotted Magpie and growled, "I thought I told you to STAY AWAY FROM HERE, and NO, I don't feel better. As a matter of fact, at this moment, I FEEL TERRIBLE!"

Pitapatpitapatpitapat. The butterflies went crazy.

They choose their parents. The chosen parent has no choice . . . but to follow the path set forth . . .

Magpie took a breath, and landed on a chamisa bush right next to the Thinking Stone.

"Skunk, I have the perfect rememdy for your arthritis."

"Since when," Skunk growled, "did I invite you to my private meditation spot and SINCE WHEN did the gabbiest beak on the desert become a . . . a MEDICINE WOMAN?"

"No, no, Skunk. Not me." Magpie shut her eyes, opened her beak and screamed, "It's KOSHARE! He's the medicine I brought to ease the pain of your arthritis."

"KO . . . who?"

"KOSHARE!"

"By any chance, you . . . you Beaky Bird," Skunk fumed, "could you be referring to that . . . MONSTER who nearly broke my back?" The sound of Skùnk's voice was as brutal as his smell.

"W-Well, as a m-matter of f-fact Skunk . . .that's exactly w-who. Oh, Skunk . . . please give him just one chance."

"GET OUT," screamed Skunk, "OUT OUT OUT!"

Magpie exploded straight up into the sky. For a split second she hovered over the thinking stone and shouted." ALL RIGHT YOU OLD CRANK. JUST WAIT AND SEE." Then she shot over the top of Three Rock Hill, spotted the shadow between the two boulders with Koshare's horns sticking out, dove down and grabbed a foothold on a dead root hanging over the side of the tallest of the two rocks. "It's time," she panted, bouncing up and down. "Run around the hill, and keep looking up until you see Skunk sitting on a big rock. DON'T SAY ANYTHING!" Magpie took a deep breath, and as she flew up into the sky, she looked back over her shoulder and shouted "Act natural. You know . . . funny. Just be yourself . . . only, exaggerate a little. Bye-bye." Then she disappeared somewhere over the top of Three Rock Hill.

Koshare clapped his hands.

BLINK!

Skunk opened his eyes. Koshare grinned, waved, jumped straight up into the sky and straddled a cloud. As the cloud swept over the Thinking Stone, Koshare stood on his head and then . . . jumped. Koshare somersaulted over and over until he landed on the desert standing on his hands. He flipped right-side-up, and waved at Skunk. Skunk gripped the edge of his Thinking Stone. His mouth was hanging open and his eyes were popping.

Koshare hobbled around on his hands and knees in a perfect charade of an arthritic old Skunk. He found a medium-size boulder and crawled to the top of it. Koshare turned his face toward the Vanishing Hills, half closed his eyes and pretended to meditate. No matter how hard Skunk tried to maintain his composure, he could not contain the laughter bursting out of his heart.

"HO HO HA HA HA. HO HO HO HA HA HA."

Koshare somersaulted to the ground opened his hands, and held them out in front of him, palms up. Four little stones leaped off the ground, landed in Koshare hands and, all by themselves, started to juggle. Every now and then one of the stones left the juggling circle, zoomed around Koshare's horns and, without missing a beat, landed back in place flying in and out, in and out of Koshare's hands. Suddenly, one of the stones, flew out of Koshare's hands, zoomed around Skunk's head, and returned to the juggler's hands.

"BRAVO," *Skunk shouted.* "BRAVO." *He shook his tail and clapped his paws.*

Koshare tossed the stones into the sky, bowed, tilted his head back and stuck out his tongue. One by one, the spinning stones dropped out of the sky and balanced on the tip of Koshare's tongue. Then, they spiraled back up into the air and disappeared inside a cloud. Koshare pretended to be surprised. He staggered backwards looking up into the sky for the little stones. Finally he stood still, held out his hands and waited for them

81

to fall out of the sky. When the little stones didn't return, Koshare looked inside the bushes. He searched the shadows and ran his fingers down the crevices of monolithic rocks. Finally, Koshare shrugged his shoulders, looked up at Skunk and mimed, "Where are my stones?"

Skunk shook his head . . . "I don't know . . ."

Koshare slumped, tilted his head to one side and looked very sad. Then, suddenly he saw something. Once again, he clapped his hands, looked at Skunk and pointed to what looked like empty space.

Koshare ran over to 'the spot' grabbed an invisible rope and shinned straight up into the sky. Skunk looked up to see if the 'rope' was attached to anything. It wasn't. The invisible 'rope' was attached to absolutely NOTHING!

The transparent rope must have started to move because Skunk saw Koshare zoom over the top of Three Rock Hill, up, up, up into the clouds and down, down down back over the Thinking Stone. "WHEEEEE," Koshare shouted as he passed by Skunk's head. "WHEEEEE" . . .Back and forth he soared over Three Rock Hill, again and again. When Koshare let go of the 'rope', he flexed his knees, put his hands together and in a perfect swan dive, landed on the desert and rolled to a stop just below the Thinking Stone. Koshare waved at Skunk, grinned and then he bowed.

"BRAVO! BRAVO! BRAVO!" Skunk pulled himself to his feet and stood on the Thinking Stone, waving his tail at The First Koshare.

For the finale, Koshare got down on his hands and knees and dug a hole in the desert. Like a coyote, he stuck his head inside the hole and sniffed. Then Koshare yelped, and yanked his head out of the hole. Clinging to the end of his nose was Dancing Desert Mouse. Koshare popped the mouse inside his mouth and pulled her tail out of his ear. When Koshare opened his mouth to speak, Skunk distinctly heard, "SQUEAK SQUEAK...SQUEAK SQUEAK...!"

Then Koshare looked all around as if to say, 'who said that?'

"HO HO HO HA HA HA," Skunk slapped his tail on the Thinking Stone. "HO HO HO HA HA HA."

Suddenly Skunk saw Dancing Desert Mouse, laughing her head off, dancing on top of Koshare's head juggling the same four stones that disap-

peared into the cloud. Koshare tried to grab her but she slipped between his fingers. Up, up, up into the clouds she soared. Koshare and Skunk searched the sky for Dancing Desert Mouse. They heard her squeaky laughter but . . . where was she?

Blink!

There she was, standing right in front of the Thinking Stone, laughing her head off. The four juggling stones, piled one on top of the other, jiggled on top of her head. "Bravo-o-o!" she squeaked. "Bravo!"

'Oh no,' Skunk gasped. 'This is unbelievable. This Koshare creature, he's absolutely. . .incredibly

. . .HILARIOUS. . .HO-HO-HO. . .BRAVO. . .HA-HA-HA. HO-HO-HO. . .BRAVO!"

As a matter of fact, Skunk laughed so hard that he fell off the Thinking Stone.

"Good gracious," gasped Magpie from her hiding place behind the Thinking Stone, "Skunk, are you all right?" Skunk lay flat on his back with all four feet waving in the air. "HA HA HA HO HO HO. Magpie, is that you?"

Magpie fluttered to the top of the thinking stone where Skunk could see her.

"Did you see. . ." giggled Skunk, "what I just saw? Dancing. . .(giggle). . .De-Desert. . .(giggle). . .Mo-Mouse. . .HA-HA-HA-HA. . .juggling. . .those. . .st-stones? HO-HO-HO-HO. Great glorious being. . .I've. HA HA. . .never. . .ever. . .in my entire life. . .laughed. . .HO HO. . .so ha-hard. . .HA HA HA HO HO HO."

"Skunk, are you OK. . .laying there on your back like that?"

"HO-HO-HO. HA-HA-HA." When Skunk could speak again, he gasped, "Funny . . . fat creature . . . with black and white stripes . . . wha-what's it called?" Skunk jabbed his paw toward the desert.

"Koshare."

"Koshare . . . yes, yes, of course. Now I remember. Koshare. Amazing. He's ABSOLUTELY . . . AMAZING! Magpie, you were right, I feel wonderful. Ever since I started laughing, I haven't had time to think one serious thought, and as for this Koshare creature, whoever he is, whatever he is . . . why, why he's is absolutely . . . HILARIOUS!"

"Why Skunk, that's . . . that's wonderful," said Magpie, panting with relief as much as from the heat. She felt a little dizzy and she stood quietly for a few moments fanning herself with one wing. "As a matter of fact, Skunk," she cooed when she felt her brain settling, "I'm absolutely delighted that you find Koshare so . . . so funny." Magpie blinked her eyes, flourished her tail feathers under Skunk's nose and hopped a little closer to the prostrate form. "By the way, ah, isn't it about time for you to stand up?"

Skunk giggled. "What an acrobat! What a CLOWN!"

"Skunk, I must confess," said Magpie, "I never saw Koshare perform quite. . .like that. Somehow, I think he senses . . . ah, that you're . . . a very special creature. Now if you'd care to stand up, I'm sure that Koshare will be delighted to assist."

"I suppose," said Skunk, peering down over his nose at his furry belly, "under the circumstances, that's an appropriate suggestion. I must look rather silly lying here on my back with my legs waving in the air." Skunk snorted, lay his head back down and giggled, "I must be a sight. . .HA HA HO HO. . .for sore eyes. . .HEE HEE HEE HA HA HA."

"Skunk, excuse me, for interrupting your laughter," said Magpie, "but I warned Koshare not to come up here unless you gave him a personal invitation so-o-o, if you don't mind . . ."

"KOSHARE-E-E-E," shouted Skunk. "Will you please come up here, right now."

"Here I am." (giggle giggle)

"Who said that?" said Skunk rolling his eyes at Magpie.

"It sounded like Koshare" replied Magpie. She looked all around but Koshare was nowhere to be seen. "He was suppose to wait for your invitation down on the desert." Magpie locked her claws around the twisted body of a silver, sun-bleached root and leaned out over the edge of Three Rock Hill as far as the root would stretch.

"BOO!"

Magpie shot straight up into the air. "KOSHARE!" she shrieked beating her wings to keep from losing her balance, "THAT WASN'T FUNNY!" She dove at Koshare's head, made a terrible shrieking noise and disappeared behind a boulder. Three black feathers zig-zagged down from the sky and settled in the middle of Skunk's welcoming belly.

"HOO-HOO-HOO. . .HA HA HA. That was hilarious. Koshare, you gave that bird quite a start. HOO-HOO-HOO . . . HA HA HA."

Koshare couldn't take his eyes off the jiggling patch of shiny black hair that covered Skunk's underbody. Ever so slowly he extended his hand until his fingers touched and lost themselves inside the soft fur.

"So this is what you look like, close up," chuckled Skunk staring at the bizarre looking creature stroking him on the belly.

"Ouuuuuuu . . . Skunk feel so-o-o good." Without any further hesitation, Koshare knelt down beside Skunk and buried his face in the luxurious forest of mid-night hair, and that's how Magpie found them when she regained enough dignity to return to the Thinking Stone.

Koshare felt her claws digging into his shoulder. He sat up and was momentarily blinded by a glare of sunlight bouncing off the horrible beak. Koshare grabbed his ear, fell backwards, and buried his head underneath his arms.

"Dat Boo," hissed Magpie through her furiously clenched beak, "wuzz NOT funny. You scared me half to death."

"Oh come now, Magpie," chuckled Skunk, "Where's your sense of humor. If you could have only seen yourself . . . HO HO HO HA HA HA . . . you'd be laughing too. HO HO HO HA HA HA." Once again Skunk gave in and laughed, and laughed, and laughed.

"Well, I'll be." Magpie stared incredulously at Skunk, and then at Koshare. She jumped off Koshare's shoulder, and skuttled back into the shadows underneath the Thinking Stone. "What is this," she muttered from the darkness, "a CONSPIRACY?" Neither Skunk or Koshare could see the tiny smile curling up one side of her beak.

"CON . . . CONS . . . Sspp-ppp . . . ?"

"A CON-SPI-RA-CY," rasped the voice of Magpie from underneath the Thinking Stone, "is when two or more creatures bond together to enjoy the misery of another creature, who, in this case, happens to be me."

"Momma's really mad," said Koshare, blinking his eyes at Skunk.

"Don't worry, she'll get over it." Skunk winked. "But I have a plan. After you've helped me get up on my feet, why don't you do something that will make Magpie laugh."

"Ok," Koshare said brightly, "I take Momma for a spin." Koshare crawled over to Skunk and eased his fingers under the knobby spine. Very gently he lifted the ancient creature into his arms, stood up and lay him down on top of the Thinking Stone.

"Thank you Koshare. Now, if you'll excuse me," Skunk yawned, "I need some time to meditate."

"Koshare play with Mama."

"MAMA?" Skunk giggled. "Come now, Koshare, Do you really believe that gossipy magpie bird, is your Mother? HO HO HO HA HA HA. Now I've heard everything. HA HA HA HEE HEE HEE."

Before another fit of laughter tumbled the legend keeper off balance he anchored his claws into the soft red sandstone, thus insuring his point of view straight across the desert into the heart of the Vanishing Hills.

Koshare somersaulted over to the shadow where Magpie dozed in the rising heat of the afternoon. He knelt down and eased his finger underneath her chest. "Mama, want to play with me?"

Magpie turned her head sideways and stared up out of the shadows into brightest pair of eyes she had ever seen. She yawned and ruffled her feathers "Now I know . . ." she mumbled under her breath, carefully clamping first one claw and then the other around the fat, worm-like claw. "I *am the First Koshare's mother.*"

Faster then the blink of an eye, Koshare jumped to his feet and off they flew.

MAGPIE'S FAINT

Out of the corner of his eye, Skunk watched Koshare leap from boulder to boulder with Magpie clutched underneath his arm. Every now and then, he'd flourish the bird over his head like a triumphant banner. Her irridecent tail feathers scattered rays of light and flashed them into Skunk's face. Ever so slowly skunk turned his body until he faced west. His eyes followed the familiar trail leading straight across the desert, and rested when they reached the cool, blue shadows of the Vanishing Hills.

As usual, the ephemeral shapes danced and shimmered, always mysterious in their illusions of coming and going. "I wonder," murmured Skunk, "if I've grown so old . . . that my life is turning into a legend right before my eyes." Skunk stared thoughtfully down his long nose resting on his paws. On a whim, he put one toe inside his mouth, nuzzled through the hair and nipped the skin. "Ouch!" A drop of blood welled up through the fur. "I'm alive," he murmured incredulously. He shook his head. "I swear I heard Koshare . . .call that magpie . . . Mama."

BLINK!

At first, New Beings are exceptionally clumsy. They crash into everything, including deserts, mountain peaks, rocks, trees and often, other creatures. By the end of the third day most New Beings have successfully completed the initial collisions with their earthly parents.

"Magpie, I heard that!" shouted Skunk assuming that somehow, the voice he heard belonged to Magpie, "I told you yesterday . . . what you know about New Beings . . .is

89

RUBBISH," Skunk rolled his paw into a fist and shook it at the sun, "DO YOU HEAR ME? TRASH AND RUBBISH. . .OWWWW!" The sharp pain in his vertebrae made Skunk gasp, "Can't you tell . . .I'm far too old . . . and arthritic . . . to be anybody's FATHER!" Very, very carefully Skunk eased himself off the Thinking Stone. "What I need," he grunted, "is a little walk to clear my head."

"LOOK SKUNK . . . LOOK AT ME! KOSHARE PLAY WITH MAMA."

Koshare made a flying leap over Skunk waving the terrified Magpie over his head. "LOOK AT ME-E-E," shouted the absolutely amazing acrobat. And when Koshare's toes touched the ground on the other side of the Thinking Stone he jetted straight up into the Blue Bowl Sky.

"Look at ME-E-E-E-e-e-e-e."

Skunk squinted his eyes and tried to follow the diminishing sound of Koshare's voice far, far up in the sky.

"Here I am."

Skunk jumped. "OU-U-UCH!"

The unmistakable sound of Koshare's voice boomed from behind the Thinking Stone. In spite of the pains running up and down in his spine, Skunk craned his head around and saw Koshare, plain as day, standing on his head behind the Thinking Stone. A pale, limp Magpie dangled underneath his arm. The New Being waved, flipped right side up, somersaulted off the stone, and once again, soared into the sky. Up, up, up he flew until he found the "sky rope" and once again, swung back and forth, across the top of Three Rock Hill.

"WHEE-E-E-E. LOOK AT ME-E-E-E-E," Koshare screamed, "SKU-U-UNK, LOOK AT ME-E-E-E." Three times Koshare swung over the Thinking Stone, before he let go of the rope, tumbled through the air and landed, feet first, on the desert below. He ran to a patch of wild daisies, snatched a bouquet and in one leap landed back on top of Three Rock Hill.

Koshare somersaulted over to Skunk and scattered the flowers across his back.

"Skunk see Koshare playing? grinned the New Being looking as fresh as the daisies clutched in his hand.

"Indeed, I did. That was SOME playing!" Skunk nodded his head in amazement. "Koshare," he chuckled, "you are absolutely . . . amazing! But tell me something . . . doesn't 'playing' . . . ever make you tired?"

"What Skunk mean . . . t-ti-red?"

"Oh." Skunk shut his eyes and thought a moment. "Now, let see. Tired means . . ." he opened his eyes, looked at Magpie clamped underneath Koshare's arm, looked away again and stared across the desert. For a moment, Skunk closed his eyes again, opened them and murmured. "Koshare, tired means . . . what Magpie is right now."

"Mama?" Koshare looked surprised. Very slowly he followed the contours of his chest downward, until he saw the limp, pale bird hanging upside down under his arm. "MAMMA!" he screamed. Koshare righted the bird and cradled her limp body in his hands. He looked at Skunk and cried. "Tired . . .make Mama look . . . AWFUL."

Skunk nodded his head, took a deep breath and let it whistle out between his teeth. "Koshare, lay Magpie down on the ground."

"Ti-ti-red bad, bad thing," Koshare whimpered.

Skunk poked his nose through Magpie's feathers until he touched her skin. "Feels mighty clammy," he mumbled, "for a hot, hot day." Then Skunk laid his ear on Magpie's chest. Pitapatpitapatpitapat. "Too fast," Skunk mumured. He looked up at Koshare and repeated, "Hearts beating, way too fast. I think she's FAINTED."

"FA-FA-FAIN-TED?" Koshare gulped. Wh-what's fa-fa . . .?"

"This isn't a classroom," Skunk snapped, "THIS IS A CRISIS!" Koshare started to cry.

"Sorry," Skunk apologized. "I . . . I didn't mean to make you cry. I just forgot . . . How can you possibly know anything about fainting." Skunk shaded Magpie with his tail. "Fainting is like a sudden attack of deep sleep. Fainting occurs when the brain. . ." Skunk pointed to his head, "doesn't get enough blood."

"Bl-bl-ood?"

"This . . " Skunk nipped his paw and again a crimson drop swelled out of the black fur, "is blood."

Koshare sobbed and watched the droplet roll off Skunk's paw into the dust. "Wh-why bl-blood leave Mama's br-br . . .?"

"BRAIN. Too much somersaulting," said Skunk matter-of-factly.

Poison arrows couldn't have inflicted any greater anguish on Koshare's heart than Skunk's blunt, but truthful answer.

"Ko-Ko-share . . . m-make MA-MA . . . f-faint?"

Skunk nodded. His tail slapped back and forth against the Thinking Stone.

"WAAAAAAA. WAAAAAAA. WAAAAAAA WAAAAAA," *Koshare wailed.* 'OHHHH NO-O-O-O. NO-O-O-O. OHHHHHH.' *Koshare groaned. Koshare moaned. His cries brought tears to every stone. The boulders trembled and the coyotes howled,* "AH-RU-U-U-U AH-RU-U-U-U *yip yip* AH-RU-U-Uuuuuuu."

"Koshare we have to move Magpie out of the sun," said Skunk. "Pick her up and follow me inside my cave."

Tenderly, oh so tenderly, Koshare lifted the pale, unconscious bird into his arms and followed Skunk inside the cave.

"Lay her down on this pile of grass and wait here until I return." Skunk disappeared into the back of the cave and returned, his tail sparkling with drops of water. He shook the water over Magpie's face and body and sat down next to Koshare. Together they watched for a change in her condition; a jerking claw, a fluttering eyelid but nothing happened.

Magpie lay as still as a leaf on a windless day.

Koshare cried and cried and cried. With one fat finger he stroked Magpie on her chest mumbling over and over again, "Koshare, bad creature . . . Koshare bad, bad creature."

"All creatures make mistakes," snapped Skunk. Koshare's morbid monotone ragged his nerves. "Putting yourself down isn't going to make Magpie wake up any sooner." Skunk's tail whipped back and forth raising a cloud of dust inside the cave. A fit of sneezing forced him outside into the fresh air. "He's driving me NUTS," Skunk muttered blowing his nose and wiping his eyes on his tail.

'. . . nuts nuts nuts,' echoed the blue and purple shadows of the Vanishing Hills. Skunk hobbled down the path leading to the Thinking Stone.

As her shadow passed over Three Rock Hill, Raven Passing By felt a twinge flutter through her heart. "Something strange is going on down there." She blinked her eyes and kept on flying toward Little Waterhole.

Gritting his teeth with pain Skunk completed the final maneuver to the top of the Thinking Stone. He turned to face the Vanishing Hills but what he saw made him hesitate before laying down. An intensity of sunlight searing the desert caused the normally still, flat surface to jiggle up and down. The shock of this unpleasant occurence caused Skunk to blink his eyes. Suddenly, the horizon snapped, its fine wire stretched beyond endurance, and for a moment, everything blew asunder: cactus, chamisa, tufts of grass, boulders, stones, pebbles, lizards, coyotes, Laughing Long-Eared Rabbits, dorment seeds, bits of root, and clouds and clouds of dust. Straight out of the sky a blast of heat spun Skunk backwards but instead of anchoring his claws into the stone, the ancient legend keeper slid down the contours of its wrinkled face, hurried down the path and with a renewed sense of humility and gratitude backed into the shelter of his cave.

"Koshare bad creature . . . Koshare bad, bad creature," moaned the wind inside the cave.

Skunk panted and waited for his eyes to adjust to the darkness. He considered telling Koshare about the unusual circumstances occuring outside, but thought better of it. "Koshare," said Skunk redirecting his attention on the bird grown even paler during his short absence, "Stop staring at Magpie as if she were dead. Instead, try to picture her flying through the sky on a sunny morning. And Koshare," Skunk added, "Forgive yourself for playing a little rough."

The afternoon wore on. Outside the cave, the desert settled, its skin miraculously falling back into the same graceful contours and subtleness of tone just as it was, before the interruption. Inside the cave: "OHHHH . . . OHHhhh . . . Koshare bad, bad creature. OHHHHHH Ohhhhhhh." Inside the cave, nothing, absolutely nothing appeared to have changed.

"Yip yip, AH-RUUUuuuuuuu," howled a sympathetic creature somewhere outside.

"SCRABBLEWUZZLEFUZZERWICK," Skunk muttered under his breath. With his tail high above his head Skunk paced around and around the tiny cavern where Koshare wailed and Magpie lay as still and white as new fallen snow.

Before the sun set, Skunk slipped outside to catch a glimpse of the painted sky. "Sku-u-unk," Koshare sobbed, "I need you. Mama l-look like n-nothing move in-side."

"Does he ever sleep?" Skunk called to the sun as it slid behind the Vanishing Hills.

"Ho ho ho ha ha ha," roared the sleepy sun slipping between the sheets of twilight hanging just below the Vanishing Hills

"Koshare," Skunk said backing into the cave. "Magpie is alive. I admit, she doesn't look so good, but she's alive. I promise."

By nightfall, Magpie still hadn't moved a feather. Long, black, finger clouds swept across the moon. Finally, much to Skunk's relief, Koshare crawled into a corner of the cave and cried himself to sleep.

When Koshare's snores fell into a steady rhythm, Skunk picked Magpie up and moved outside the cave. He leaned his head against the rocks, watched the moon and listened to the coyotes:
"AH-RU-U-U-U *yip yip* AH-RU-U-U-Uuuuuuu.
We sing the songs of stars.
We listen to the wind
We hear our ancestors . . . calling, calling.
AH-RU-U-U-U *yip yip* AH-RU-U-U-Uuuuuuu."
And this is where Skunk drifted off to sleep, with Magpie cradled in his arms.

95

WAY TAY SAY

BLINK!

Skunk jerked awake and grabbed Magpie just before she slid to the ground. He nestled her against his furry chest for the early morning air was icy cold. "Paler," he murmured, "this bird looks m-much, m-much p-p-paler." Skunk's teeth chattered and his body shook in the pre-dawn chill. He poked his nose underneath Magpie's feathers. "C-c-cold. This b-body feels m-much t-too c-cold." Skunk turned his head to one side and lay his ear on Magpie's chest. "Pit a pat a-pit a . . .pat . . ." Hurriedly Skunk half-dragged, half-carried Magpie inside the cave, this unwelcomed activity causing Skunk's recalcitrant vertebrae to crunch and grind. "OWWWW!" Skunk gasped. He clapped his paw over his mouth so as not awaken Koshare. "Unmerciful bones," Skunk muttered. "Right now, I have no time, for your complaints. This bird is nearly . . ." Skunk let his thought drift off into the frozen darkness and put his full attention on dragging Magpie inside the cave. "I've got to do something . . ." he muttered, "I don't know what, but whatever it is, I've got to do it . . . FAST!"

Skunk lay Magpie down on a pile of dry grass and covered her with the extra tufts scattered about the floor. He hurried to the rear of the cave and held his tail against the thin layer of ice covering the rock wall. Some droplets of water beaded into the hair and in a few minutes Skunk was worming his way back through the clutter of rocks toward the cavern where Magpie lay.

BLINK!

Through the opening at the end of the short, curving passage, something flashed and a light as bright as the sun beamed straight into Skunk's face. "Wha-whats g-going on?" gasped Skunk. His heart began to pound and a rush of blood surged through his body. He felt weak and dizzy. He shut his

97

eyes, inhaled, and let the air out slowly. When he regained his balance, he dared to peek around a boulder into the cavern where he had left Magpie lying on the grass. What he saw he could not believe. With both eyes popping Skunk gulped and gasped. "WAY TAY SAY!"

More stunned than afraid, Skunk covered his face and withdrew behind the rock. When he dared look again he stared into a light far brighter than the sun, yet somehow the quality of this light allowed the eye to remain wide open. A huge white coyote stood over Magpie, licking her and breathing light into her body. One forepaw gently rolled the bird from side to side. In and out each tiny claw, underneath and in between each feather of her wings, chest, and back; up and down the sweeping tail Way Tay Say primed the tiny body back to life.

"I know I'm dead," said Skunk. A beatific smile spread across his face. "By the grace of Way Tay Say, this humble cave has turned into the mountain of eternal light." Skunk's wet tail sank to the ground. He shut his eyes, crossed his paws over his chest and assumed the final pose of a body without its soul. "Way Tay Say . . . Great Spirit of Life," Skunk mumbled, "thank you for greeting Magpie and me into this heavenly mountain of light. I see you waking Magpie from her transitional flight and now, I too, await your welcome."

Suddenly another voice of Skunk, an irreverent intruder, blurted out, "Hold everything." Skunk shoved a toe inside his mouth and nipped the skin. "OU-U-UCH!" howled Skunk's regular voice. A drop of blood welled up through the thick, black hair. "How . . . how can this be?" he gasped. "M-my own r-real b-b-blood . . .and W-Way T-Tay S-Say?" Skunk's eyes darted back and forth between the glowing coyote and his bleeding paw. One by one, the crimson drops rolled off his paw and plopped into the dust. Then everything dissolved in light.

BLINK!

A strange sound, like whirring thunder filled the cave.

"I am alive," gasped Skunk the legend keeper. "Well, b-bless my s-soul." Skunk watched the tiny pool of blood drying into a dark red stain. "My blood," he murmured. In a few moments, Skunk's long nose inched around the boulder followed by two shiny, jet black eyes.

"T-that's really W-Way Tay S-Say . . out there." Skunk steadied himself against the rock. His eyes rolled up inside his head and his legs began to shake. "A-At this v-very instant," Skunk babbled, "W-Way Tay Say is l-licking . . . M-Magpie, and I'm . . .I'm a l-living w-witness." Skunk gasped, ". . . t-to a m-miracle."

Thus, late in life, Skunk the legend keeper of the Vanishing Hills, came into his full spiritual blooming. Early that morning, Way Tay Say revealed to Skunk, inside a cave on Three Rock Hill, that our eternal spirit, is just as real as blood.

A noisy yawn from the back of the cave, followed by the sound of smacking lips shattered Skunk's moment of bliss. Skunk's heart somersaulted, and his eyes darted back and forth between the shadows in the rear of the cave and Way Tay Say standing over Magpie.

"Oh no," muttered Skunk, "K-Koshare's awake. "W-what am I g-going to d-do when he see: . . . when he sees . . . all this l-light," Skunk gulped, "n-not t-to m-mention . . . Way T-Tay S-Say . . . l-licking . . . licking his . . m-mother?" Skunk shudered and held his breath.

In a moment, two black and white zig-zag horns poked through the shadows and Koshare, blinking his eyes and yawning, emerged into the light.

MAMA?"

"SHHHHHHHH!" Skunk scuttled over to Koshare and

pointed to Way Tay Say. To Skunk's utter sruprise, instead of screams of horror, a light similar to the glow in Magpie's wide open eyes, flashed across the utterly foolish face of the First Koshare.

"GA?"

BLINK! *The cave darkened and suddenly Magpie was up on her feet shaking bits of grass out of her feathers.*

"Why is everybody staring at me?" asked Magpie.

Koshare and Skunk exchanged looks of astonishment and continued to gawk.

"You two sure look silly," said Magpie stretching first one wing and then the other. "My mother always told me that if your mouth hangs open long enough, the bugs'll fly in." Magpie giggled. "Good advice for a bird, but rather unpleasant, I would think, for a skunk and a New Being." Then Magpie opened her beak and rolled her eyes at Koshare and Skunk. Enjoying her little charade, she giggled again and with a saucy flip of her, once again resplendent tail, she turned around, hopped out of the cave and fluttered into a bush. "How beautiful the crimson sky of morning," trilled Magpie in a squeaky voice definitely not suited for higher notes. "Thank you Sun, for bringing forth another splendid day," warbled Magpie, The Resurrected.

Inside the cave Koshare and Skunk winced and clapped their hands over their ears.

When her song was done Magpie hopped to the entrance of the cave and shouted, "Hey, you two, the sun's up and I'm leaving for my early morning breakfast flight. See you later. Bye-bye."

"YIPPEE," Koshare shouted. He crawled outside the cave, stood up and waved at Magpie as she circled over Three Rock Hill.

"BYE-BYE MOMMA, BYE-BYE."

With a twinkle in her eye, Magpie turned around and flew past Koshare's face. She touched his forehead with her wings and whispered, "Behave yourself, and mind your FATHER." Then up she soared straight up, up, up into the Blue Bowl Sky.

"FA-FA . . .?"

Koshare stood and waved until Magpie disappeared from sight. Then he scratched his head.

"FA . . .FA-thh . . . Fa-thh . . .? What's FATH-ER?"

A little breeze carrying the scents of sage and chamisa wafted up Koshare's nose. And when a flight of bluebirds swept across the top of Three Rock Hill, Koshare followed them in a jubilee of somersaults, headstands, and triple gainers.

"YIPPEE!" he shouted. "YIPPEE."

Koshare jumped clear over the top of Three Rock Hill trailing a rainbow behind him. A long distance from Three Rock Hill, a tongue of lightning flickered in and out the blue and purple shadows of the Vanishing Hills.

Skunk backed out of the cave and hobbled down the ancient trail leading to the Thinking Stone. Sleeping outside in the cold air hadn't agreed with his arthritis. "Me, an ordinary creature of the earth," Skunk mumbled, "and right before my eyes . . . Way Tay Say." The vertebrae crunched. Skunk stopped and rode the spasms. Daggers flickered, stabbed and twisted. Skunk shouted, "Hooray. Hooray. Magpie lives! WAY TAY SAY!" Then he shut his eyes, recalled the light and breathed deeply. In a matter of minutes the pains subsided, and Skunk continued walking down the path. When he reached his destination, instead of climbing to his regular meditating groove, he leaned against a lower boulder on the sunny side of the Thinking Stone and bathed in the warming light.

Before long Skunk's thoughts rested on the clouds sweeping across the wide expanse of Blue Bowl Sky on their journey to oblivion behind the Vanishing Hills.

"Sku-unk?"

BLINK! Skunk opened his eyes. "Hello Koshare."

"Skunk?"

Skunk rubbed his eyes and yawned. "Yes, yes, what can I do for you this morning?"

"Mama still OK?"

"Koshare, you saw Magpie this morning. Now why ask such a silly question?"

"Skunk?"

"Yes, Koshare."

"Where bright-light creature hide?" Koshare scanned the top of Three Rock Hill as if he expected to see a glowing coyote face peeking out from behind a boulder.

"Koshare," Skunk chuckled, "that bright light creature. . . that's Way Tay Say. You'll never find him hiding behind a rock. You don't realize how rarely Way Tay Say makes an appearance as the glowing, white coyote that you saw this morning. Most of the time, Way Tay Say is invisible."

Koshare looked confused.

"Invisible means something that you can't see with your eyes. Many forms of life are too small for us to see. Creatures such as: amoebas, quarks, atoms, and neutrinos are examples of such phenomenona. Most of the time, Way Tay Say, has no form at all, however that invisible spirit is the essence generating all forms of life, both visible and invisible. The strange thing is that the invisible Way Tay Say, is the only aspect of ouselves and our existence that's lasting and real.

Everything else, Koshare, believe it or not, is temporary, a wonderful and terrifying dance comprised only of dreams and illusions. Now listen carefully, for there is more to this extraordinary story. Way Tay Say dreams alive our planet earth within the universe of this same dreaming. But, Koshare," Skunk's voice dropped to an impassioned whisper, "the strangest and most miraculous thing of all is that only creatures awakening from the illusions of their worldly dreams are able to see Way Tay Say as the glowing white coyote we saw this morning."

For a few minutes Koshare sat quietly chewing on one of his horns. Finally he asked, "Skunk, Way Tay Say inside STARS?"

"Yup, even inside the stars. Koshare, Way Tay Say is The One spiritual dreamer within us all illuminating this entire universe of stars, planets and moons. Here, on Earth, the sun is our mother/father star. We share our sun with our eight siblings: Mercury, Venus, Mars, Saturn, Pluto, Jupiter, Uranus and Neptune. On earth: clouds, coyotes, dragonflies, snakes, trees, bats, rocks, mountains and butterflies exist because the dream of Way Tay Say imagines and creates such miracles. Koshare, Way Tay Say dreams EVERYTHING, including . . . YOU!"

"Me too?"

Skunk smiled. "You too. And you know what?"

Koshare solemnly shook his head from side to side.

"I have a strong feeling," continued Skunk, his voice raised barely above a whisper, "that someday you, Koshare, might become . . . a big, BIG dreaming . . ."

Koshare stared at his feet and wiggled his toes. "Way Tay Say glowed brighter than all the stars, didn't he Skunk?"

"Way Tay Say, is The One brightest light that is."

"Way Tay Say sure is a big, BIG, bright IN-IN-VIS-S-SIBLE thing," said Koshare stretching his arms as wide as he could.

Skunk nodded and added, "Way Tay Say, is The One light

that illuminates this universe out of darkness. Way Tay Say is the creator of light within the darkness; Way Tay Say is life and death and life revitalized . . . just like your momma."

Koshare stared across the desert and watched the shadows of the Vanishing Hills dance across the horizon.

"Koshare," Skunk continued, "You are only four days old, and already you've seen a miracle, the likes of which I had to live a long, long time to witness. Magpie's life must be of great importance to Way Tay Say. Why else, pray tell, would the illuminating coyote spirit have come to Magpie's rescue this morning and helped her spirit return to earth?"

Koshare sat quietly and paid close attention to every word of Skunk's long, long story.

"Remember Koshare, its only under very unusual cir-cumstances," Skunk repeated, "that Way Tay Say appears to living creatures in the form of a white coyote."

"What's . . . un-un-uzzal cir-cir . . ."

"Unusual circumstances," explained Skunk, "occur when regular dreamed events unfold to a peak in time when living creatures, like you and me, are able penetrate the illusions of our worldly existence and experience, through our bodies, the reality of our spiritual being. Seeing Way Tay Say in coyote form Koshare, that's an unusual circumstance. Watching Way Tay Say help Magpie bring her spirit back into her earthly body, Koshare, that's a miracle. Essentially unusual circumstances and miracles, are the same thing. Creatures," Skunk grinned, "like me . . . always act surprised when miracles occur."

"I wasn't sur-surprised," said Koshare, "I was just happy that mama woke up!"

"I could see how happy you were," replied Skunk. "Koshare, I don't suppose that you are aware of this, but, your smile, ah . . . is as brilliant as the light of Way Tay Say, when you're very happy."

Koshare smiled and once more Skunk was dazzled by the

light of ten thousand stars.

"By the way," said Skunk rubbing his eyes, "I wonder where Magpie is?" While Skunk searched for a speck of black inside the empty, bluest, brightest bowl of blue, Koshare noticed a sudden tightening in the features of Skunk's narrow face.

"Koshare," said Skunk, "there's something we need to discuss before Magpie returns."

"'bout stars?"

"No. Not about stars. We have BUSINESS to discuss. Koshare, do you know what a SECRET is?" Skunk looked straight at Koshare. His tail shot straight up over his head. The white tip trembled over so slightly.

"Se-se-cret? . . . Koshare frowned and scratched his head.

"A secret," explained Skunk, "is something you hide from somebody else." Skunk's eyes, bright and glittering, pointed straight into Koshare's face. "You and I have a secret that we must hide from Magpie. Our secret concerns Way Tay Say and all these miracles.

"What SEE-CRET for?"

"Because . . . because of The Tradition."

"What's tra-tra . . .?"

"Koshare, right now, I haven't time to explain the meaning of legendary traditions. "Skunk eyes worried the sky, and his tail switched back and forth as if it were swatting flies. "Now listen carefully to what I'm telling you. Magpie doesn't remember one thing, from the time she fainted until she woke up this morning, just after Way Tay Say vanished. So, Koshare, you see, Magpie has no idea that . . . that she nearly died, or that Way Tay Say ever appeared inside the cave."

At the mention of the word, 'faint', and the reminder of his mother's close call with death Koshare's face collapsed. His head dropped between his hands, and he moaned. "Koshare bad creature. Koshare bad, bad, creature."

"Good gracious Koshare, please . . .don't start that again."

Skunk's whole body jittered. "LOOK . . ." Skunk shouted into Koshare's ear. "MAGPIE'S ALIVE! I'M ALIVE! YOU'RE ALIVE! Besides all that, don't you realize you're an extraordinary creature who only needs to remember one thing?"

Koshare slowly lifted his head and blinked at Skunk.

"Now what is it that you need to remember?"

"SEE-CRET!" shouted Koshare jumping to his feet and clapping his hands over his head.

"BRAVO!" Skunk applauded and waved his tail. "Now, tell me, what is our secret?"

Koshare leaned down and shouted, "Koshare see Way Tay Say and Way Tay Say make MIR-MIR-ACLES!"

Skunk nodded. "Good, Koshare. That's part of our secret. Now what else is there to remember about our secret?"

Koshare gulped, bit his lip, and whispered, "Koshare never tell momma . . . 'bout fainting."

"BRAVO, Koshare. That's very, very good." Skunk, grabbed his tail and tickled Koshare's cheek. "All you need to remember, is to never, never, NEVER tell our secret to another creature, especially Koshare, especially to your Mother. Do you promise?"

"I promise."

Thus, on the fourth day of Koshare's life on earth, Skunk the legend keeper and story teller of his time, introduced Koshare to the most faithfully guarded tradition of the Vanishing Hills, that being as follows: any creature who sees Way Tay Say, must never speak to another about the incident, unless the other creature has shared the same vision.

"Skunk.
"Yes Koshare."
"I'm hungry."

"Well, go find something to eat," said Skunk who was in need of a nap and inadequately prepared to handle such a phenomenon as feeding The First Koshare. "Where is that Magpie anyway? Seems like she's been gone an awfully long time."

"Momma hunting grasshoppers."

"Oh, well, if that's all . . ." Skunk's eyelids dropped over his eyes. He yawned and said. "Koshare, help me up to the top of this Thinking Stone. Right now, I need a little time to gather my thoughts. You run off and play, or eat, or whatever it is that children do when their parents need time to think."

Skunk yawned again, wrapped his tail around his feet, and closed his eyes. "Magpie was right," Skunk thought. "We're marked. What else can it be? Magpie, myself and this extraordinary Koshare creature. I suppose," Skunk yawned again, "That under such exceptionally unusual circumstances, that it's entirely possible for an elderly, legend keeper and retired storyteller such as I, to be . . . the First Koshare's . . . father."

BLINK!

FAMILY

"Skunk?"

Skunk's tail shot up. His eyes snapped open. "Oh," Skunk sighed. "it's only you."

"I'm through eating."

Skunk closed his eyes and the great striped tail fluttered to the ground.

"Have you seen my Momma?"

Skunk opened his eyes again and stared up at a dirty face. Bits of leftover breakfast leaf clung to the big, red lips and fluttered every time Koshare moved his mouth. Skunk cleared his throat and ignoring Koshare's question embarked upon, what seemed to him, a far more significant issue. "Koshare, there's something I need to tell you about skunks."

"'Bout you?"

"About me, and any other skunk you may encounter on your worldly travels. Koshare, never, never startle skunks especially if they are sleeping. You aren't aware of this, but a moment ago, I . . . I almost sprayed. And as you already know, when a skunk sprays, every creature in the vicinity suffers, including the skunk.

Koshare's eyes opened wide. He jumped backwards and in his hurry to get away from Skunk, he tripped over his feet and started to roll. Just like a tumbleweed, Koshare spun all over the top of Three Rock Hill which, of course, made Skunk laugh and laugh and laugh. A cloud of dust followed Koshare everywhere he went. The humorless vertebrae ground their discs beneath the resplendent stripe of white, but Skunk's laughter was insuperable.

"Koshare," Skunk yelled when he stopped laughing. "Get back up on your feet and look at me."

Koshare picked himself up out of the dust, jumped on top

of a boulder and glowered at Skunk. Nothing smelled.

"I thought you were going to stink," Koshare yelled.

"Tell me something, Koshare. Where's my tail?"

"Hanging behind you."

"Right you are. Now, remember this. When the tail is down, a skunk can't spray."

Koshare took his time returning to the Thinking Stone. Every few minutes he'd sniff the air which only made him sneeze, for the air was still thick with particles of dust and sparkling mica bits.

"Koshare, stop sniffing and hurry over here," giggled Skunk.

"You frightened me," whined Koshare.

"I was only explaining how a skunk's mechanism of self-preservation works. Your mind jumped to conclusions and misguided you into thinking that I was actually going to spray."

"Momma tell me," murmured Koshare, slumping down and leaning his head against the Thinking Stone "'bout how Skunk stink."

"Now, in answer to your original question, no, Koshare, I haven't seen your mother since she left early morning."

Koshare looked up at the sky. His mouth drooped. "I want my Mamma."

"Well, Koshare, perhaps grasshoppers aren't as plentiful out here as they are in other places," said Skunk, looking anxiously for a dark spot moving against the flat blue face of empty space.

"I WANT MY MOMMA" sobbed Koshare suddenly collapsing into an uncontrollable fit of tears.

"Where is that confounded bird?" muttered Skunk. "And what am I suppose to do with him sitting down there crying his heart out for that . . . that gossiping bird?" Skunk scratched his fleas and stared across the desert. Koshare sobbed and sobbed. Great glistening teardrops splashed down the rocks and formed a puddle by Koshare's feet.

"Koshare, by any chance," said Skunk whose tender heart

was not designed to bear the suffering of others, "have you forgotten something, VERY IMPORTANT?"

In a minute Koshare's weeping turned into hiccups which ultimately became a runny nose. After a few good swipes at the stream with the back of his hand, Koshare stood up and looked at Skunk. He laid a grubby finger on his lips . . . "Shhhhhhhhh." He looked around to see if anyone was listening. Then the tear-stained, dust-streaked creature leaned over the ancient legend keeper and sprayed the magic word, "s-s-s-s-s-secret," into his left ear.

"BRAVO!" shouted Skunk wrinkling up his nose and shaking the flotsam and jetsam leftovers of Koshare's breakfast off his face and out of his ear. "That's right Koshare, you and I have a . . ." Skunk carefully innunciated the magic word . . . "S E C R E C T!"

A blur of feathers flashed past Skunk's nose. Koshare jumped and so did Skunk. Up went the tail and suddenly, there was Magpie standing in front of the Thinking Stone with a grasshopper hanging from her beak . . .

"MOMMA!"

The vertebrae crunched and again, Skunk's tail came fluttering down.

"Wh-where'd you come from?" gulped Skunk scrambling to regain his composure. "D-don't you remember, you . . . you . . . Gabbling Gossip, I . . . I HATE SURPRISES!"

"I came from the sky, from the sky," chirruped Magpie smiling at Koshare and ignoring Skunk's bad humor. The grasshopper leaped to its freedom. "I came from the sky, sky, sky," sang the ever-so-cheerful bird. Magpie batted her eyes at Skunk, flicked her tail under his nose, and then eyeballed the bright green escapee clinging to a blade of grass. Magpie turned her head sideways, aimed, opened her beak, and snap, down went the grasshopper to its final demise. Koshare, facinated by the process, watched the hindlegs wiggle as it went down her throat.

"I know you came from the sky," grunted Skunk praying that Magpie hadn't heard the 'magic' word. "What I mean is," he gulped grasping for a succulent train of thought that would distract Magpie's mind, "w-where did you find that grasshopper that you just swallowed?"

"What do you care where I find my meals," teased Magpie. Her tail feathers flashed in the sunlight. She sidled closer to the Thinking Stone and giggled, "Anyway, here I am, with my gullet stuffed and rarin' to go." She stretched her wingtip until it tickled Skunk's nose.

Koshare jumped up and plopped himself between Magpie and Skunk. "I missed my Momma," he said, grinnind broadly at Magpie.

"Why Koshare, what a nice thing for you to say. Do you know something, I missed you too." Magpie flew up to Koshare's shoulder and gave him a gentle peck on the cheek.

"Mama still feel good?" asked Koshare.

"Never felt better in my life, thank you Koshare," replied Magpie.

"Mama?" Koshare shot a sideways glance at Skunk who was grooming his tail, and apparently not listening to the conversation.

"Yes, Koshare."

"Mama ever think Koshare . . . bad creature?" A gust of wind grabbed Koshare's words and flung them out across the desert.

"What, Koshare? What'd you say?"

Koshare clapped his hand over his mouth and mumbled into Magpie's ear, "Mama think Koshare bad creature?"

Another gust of wind spun Magpie away from Koshare's face. She scrambled to her feet and squawked, "Nasty wind up here. Bad, Koshare? Did you say . . . BAD?"

Skunk's tail slapped back and forth against the Thinking Stone, and Koshare jumped to his hands and knees prepared to sprint.

"Nasty wind," repeated Magpie shaking the dust out of her

feathers. "Now Koshare in answer to that silly question, NO! How's that! NO, I DON'T THINK YOU'RE BAD. Troublesome perhaps. Aggravating, definately . . . but bad? . . . .NO, not . . . BAD."

Once again, Skunk's face disappeared inside his tail. And, once more Koshare sat down next to Magpie.

"Mama?"

"Yes Koshare."

"Did you ever go somersaulting with me?" A slight breeze ruffled the white stripe of hair along Skunk's back.

"Somersaulting . . . with you?" Magpie laughed. "Now whatever would possess me to something as ridiculous as . . . hey . . . hey, wait a minute." A wisp of memory, passed through her eyes and Magpie drew into herself, leaned back on her tail and thought. In a few moments she replied, "You know, now that you mention it, Koshare . . . for some reason, I do remember . . . something . . .like . . ."

"Fainting?" whimpered Koshare covering his face with his hands.

"Ummmmm." To nobody in particular, magpie murmured, "How wonderful it was . . .floating through the air . . .with you, Koshare. Why, I never moved a feather. I felt *wonn-n-n-n-derful* and . . . and, Koshare . . . do you know what? I felt like I was *filled with light*. Yes, imagine that . . . I was . . . *filled with light.*"

During this whole conversation Skunk had been eavesdropping under the camouflage of his tail, and to his surprise, each time Magpie said '*filled with light*' the same quality of light that identified the presence of Way Tay Say flooded the face of Magpie.

Magpie fluttered up to Koshare's shoulder, threw her wings around his neck and whispered, "Do you know what, Koshare, when I was flying with you, I felt as if I had as much light inside me as . . . as THE SUN."

Koshare opened his mouth and gawked at his mother.

"Like a cloud we drifted across the desert and when we

came to the Vanishing Hills we dropped down into the shadows and then . . . and then suddenly, the light disappeared, except . . ." Magpie stopped and thought a moment, "except . . for the light of the sun rising above Three Rock Hill." Magpie's feathers fired purple, green and ebony and her radiant smile beamed straight through Koshare's face. "Incredible," she whispered, "Koshare, flying with you was . . .absolutely . . incredible." Magpie glowed with maternal pride. "My, my, my Koshare," said Magpie trembling ever so slightly, "you've turned out to be an ABSOLUTELY . . . MAGNIFICENT flyer."

"But Mama," cried Koshare, "D-don't you remember anything 'bout FAINTING!"

Up shot the tail. "WHO SAID THAT?" Skunk roared.

"NOT ME!" shouted Koshare, taking off as fast as he could run across the top of Three Rock Hill. Magpie shot a long way up into the sky before she leveled off. She opened her eyes and dared to sniff. Nothing. She dropped her altitude and circled around the Thinking Stone. "WHAT'S BOTHERING YOU?" Magpie shouted at Skunk.

"KOSHARE," Skunk roared, "HAVE YOU ANY MORE QUESTIONS TO ASK YOUR MOTHER?" His tail had not stopped quivering.

"N-no" stuttered Koshare from behind a boulder located as far away from the Thinking Stone as the limited circumference of Three Rock Hill allowed.

"Koshare, please come over here, right now," yelled Skunk. Koshare noted that the tail was dropping.

A sheepish Koshare emerged from behind the boulder and slowly walked across the top of Three Rock Hill.

Before Magpie landed in a bush next to the Thinking Stone, Koshare heard her say, "Will someone please tell me what's going on around here?" Her eyes darted back and forth between Koshare and Skunk. "Koshare, answer me. Did you, or did you not ask me something . . . about fainting?"

Koshare stared at his feet. "I forgot," he mumbled.

"You forgot. YOU FORGOT?" Magpie looked confused. "I don't understand how it is possible for a brand New Being to know anything about fainting, and besides . . ." Magpie fluttered up to Koshare's shoulder and sidled up to his ear, ". . . fainting, and that magnificent flight we were discussing a few minutes ago . . .those two things, Koshare, have nothing, absolutely nothing . . in common."

Koshare continued to stare at his feet. "Nothing . . .in common," he mumbled, "ab-ab-solutely . . . NOTHING."

Magpie flew off Koshare's shoulder and settled on the Thinking Stone. "What a strange conversation this is, don't you agree Skunk? Me . . . faint? HUMPH!" Magpie huffed her feathers and grumbled, "I never heard of such a thing." Then she turned her head sideways and squinted at the sun. "PHEW. It's getting hot out here." Without another word, Magpie dropped into the shadows underneath the Thinking Stone.

For a long time, nobody said a word. Skunk turned his eyes toward the Vanishing Hills and Koshare sat on the ground drawing pictures in the dust.

Time passed. Skunk squinted one eye at the sun, and unfurled his tail from around his feet. "Now," he announced, "it's time for some shade and a little nap before supper. How would you two like to join me inside my cave. We are family, now, are we not?"

"Well, I'll be," giggled Magpie. She hopped out of her shadow into the sunlight and winked at Koshare.

"FA . . .FAM . . .LEE?" What's that?" asked Koshare looking up from his dusty sketching pad.

"A family," said Skunk, slowly adjusting his vertebrae into a compromising position, " . . .a family is a group of creatures who share a single cave. One purpose of a family is to raise children."

"Chil-drun?"

"Koshare . . ." said Skunk demonstrating the art of patience, "You're the child. Magpie is your female parent; the mother . . . and I . . ." Skunk pretended to ignore Magpie's giggles, "I . . . am your FATHER."

"FA-THER?" Koshare stood up and looked at Skunk, "What's FA-THER?"

"The father is the masculine parent whose job it is to guide the child along the path of our ancestral heritage. It is also the father's job to teach the child how to protect itself from its natural predators. A father makes sure his child learns the ancestral legacy precisely as it is dreamed by Way Tay Say." Skunk looked at Koshare, winked, waved his tail, and smiled.

"WHOOPIE-E-E," shouted Koshare. "You're my f-fa-father." He leaned across the Thinking Stone picked up Skunk and hugged him to his chest.

CRE-E-EAK. The calcified old vertebrae simply couldn't handle so much happiness and so they had to crunch. But Skunk was so happy that he hardly felt the pain.

With Skunk, the father, tucked carefully underneath his arm, Koshare skipped over to Magpie and put his finger under her chest. Once again, she hopped aboard and hitched up to his shoulder.

Raven Passing By watched The First Koshare dance all around the top of Three Rock Hill. He carried Skunk, The Legend Keeper and retired storyteller, under his left arm and Magpie, the former desert gossip, rode proudly on his shoulder. All together they sang the family song:

HAY HAY YEA-AH
We praise this day,
HEA-AH
Our hearts are filled with joy,

HEA-AH
This is our family day,
HEA-AH . . AH . . ."

"Ah-woooooooooooooo. Ar Ara-woooooooooooooo . . ."
"Oh my goodness," gasped Magpie, grabbing Koshare
around the neck, "W-what's that?"
"Ah-wooooooooooooo Ar Ara-woooooooooooooo."
"Be-e-u-tee-ful," extolled Koshare.
"Ummmmmm. Magnificent," extolled Skunk.
"S-s-scary," stuttered Magpie fluttering to the top of
Koshare's head. She wrapped her wings around one of the
floppy horns and scanned the desert for the mysterious
singer.
"It always m-makes me n-nervous" chattered Koshare's
Mother, "w-when I hear strange v-voices that I c-can't id-d-
dentify."
Skunk and Koshare exchanged smiles, and then Skunk said,
"Now, Magpie, it's probably just another lonely coyote howling
for it's lover. Come now, its time to go inside the cave. . ."
"B-but t-that . . . v-voice . . . its INCREDIBLE!"
Koshare felt Magpie shaking.
"I can almost assure you, my dear," said Skunk winking at
Koshare, "that in a very short time, our mysterious singer will
move on to other deserts." Skunk yawned, "I'm getting awful-
ly sleepy."

*One by one, they filed into the cave; Skunk, Magpie and the First
Koshare. But Skunk never got his nap because there were far too many
family matters to discuss.*

"Koshare," said Magpie. "Please put your stones and drawing sticks, all together, in this corner of the cave."

"Skunk, can I lay my grass bed next to yours?"

"Skunk, I need a little time for gossping. Could you please watch Koshare in the mornings?"

"Koshare, your father and I both agree. You've got to keep your spider pets outside our cave."

"Don't you think we should eat our supper, together, just before sunset?"

"I'll teach Koshare his legends in the morning . . ."

"We'll have to keep a close watch over Koshare until he learns his way around this desert."

"Momma, can I draw pictures on the walls of the cave?"

"I suppose we should introduce Koshare to the owl and coyote children living in the arroyo next to Little Water Hole."

"Skunk don't you think one story is enough, before bedtime?"

But during that night, the first night of the Family Celebration, Magpie, Skunk and The First Koshare danced and sang until after midnight.

"HAY HAY YAH
HAY HAY YAH
"Mama, Poppa, The First Koshare,
We are FAMILY.
HAY HAY YAH-AH-AH-AH!"

Raven-Passing-By watched the celebration on top of Three Rock Hill. Raven -Passing-By, the omnipresent witness of this dreamed and dreaming universe, watched, listened and remembered . . . everything.

LO-KA-REE

The next evening after their supper Magpie and Skunk met at the Thinking Stone to watch the sunset. Koshare was sitting on the ground on the other side of Three Rock Hill, examining a large rock.

"Sky inside this rock," Koshare whispered excitedly. He rubbed his fingers back and forth along the streaks of sky blue sediment. "Maybe the whole sky comes out of here, and . . . and then goes . . . up there."

Just as Koshare looked up into the sky Magpie appeared, flying low. "Koshare," she yelled, "run to the Thinking Stone. Skunk has something he wants to show you."

"Momma, come look and see what I found," Koshare shouted, pointing to the rock lying between his legs.

"I can't look now Koshare. Come, we must hurry to the Thinking Stone. What Skunk wants to show you only lasts for a little while."

"But Momma, wait," shouted Koshare standing up and beckoning his mother back. "Sky inside this rock. I can't just leave it lying here all by itself. I have to carry it home for safekeeping and besides, won't Poppa want to see the rock where all the sky begins?"

Magpie, not being a patient bird, was already out of hearing distance and so Koshare lifted the heavy stone onto his shoulders and started to weave his way through the scratch weed, dry grass, rocks and boulders scattered across the face of Three Rock Hill. "I just can't . . . hurry," he puffed, "no matter what Momma says. Blue Sky Stone . . . very heavy."

In a few minutes Magpie came back. Her iridescent tail flashed against the orange and crimson sky. "KOSHARE," she shouted diving toward the New Being's head, "DROP THAT ROCK!"

121

"NO," grunted Koshare. He continued staggering along just as if his mother hadn't given the command. "Sky . . . grow out of here. Got . . . to . . . got to . . . take care of Blue Sky place," Koshare puffed. "MOMMA, LOOK!" Koshare stopped walking and let the rock fall off his shoulders and thump to the ground. "SEE?" Koshare pointed to the blue streaks racing through the stone.

Magpie, succumbing to Koshare plea, landed on top of the rock, turned her head sideways and looked. "Koshare," she giggled in spite of herself, "that's not Sky. Those blue streaks are turquoise. Turquoise is a beautiful blue stone that grows inside the earth."

"Not sky?" murmured Koshare pointing to the streaks of blue. "Tur-tur-quoise . . . not sky?"

"Sky is . . ." Magpie thought a moment, "sky is invisible, empty space that only looks blue, like turquoise. Sky doesn't come out of anything. Its just, kind of, always there, like the sun, moon and the stars. Speaking of which, now, will you put this rock on top of this crooked boulder where you can find it in the morning and run, as fast as you can, to the Thinking Stone. I promise, Skunk has something to show you that you will like as much as turquoise."

"Promise?"

"I promise. Hurry now, because Skunk's surprise only lasts a little while. Stones, Koshare, even those as beautiful as turquoise, last forever."

Once again Koshare hauled the rock up to his shoulder and for safekeeping, rolled it onto a ledge inside a giant crone of stone, whose humps and bumps, miraculously balanced and adhered, thrust her higher into the sky than the neighboring monoliths formed more sensibly than she. Once released of his treasure, Koshare, leapfrogged, boulder to boulder across the top of Three Rock Hill. A final jump placed him directly in front of the Thinking Stone.

"Here I am," chirruped Koshare from inside a cloud of dust.

"AH-CHOO! So I see." Skunk coughed and wiped his eyes. "Now, quickly, turn around and look at the sky, and tell me what you see."

Koshare turned around and squinted his eyes through the swirl of mica and flying sand. Koshare noticed a barely visible point of light glowing above the Vanishing Hills. As the dust settled, the glowing grew brighter. Koshare looked over his shoulder at Skunk and pointed excitedly at the light. "STAR-R-R," he gasped. "One beauty-ful star-r-r."

"Tonight, Koshare," said Skunk, "your bedtime story is about that star."

"Star story!" Koshare clapped his hands, stood on his head and kicked his feet in the air. "Star-r-r stor-r-r-ry, Star-r-r stor-r-r-ry," sang The First Koshare. "R's" rolled, one by one, out of the bright red lips and tumbled plink, plank, plink all the way to the bottom of Three Rock Hill.

"One star story, and then bedtime," said Magpie looking sternly at Koshare.

"In my wildest dreams," Skunk mused shutting his eyes for a moment, "I never would have imagined that a magpie, especially this one, would end up being the First Koshare's mother. Surprises, hmmmmm. These days, Way Tay Say's dreams are certainly full of surprises. Now that I've become the First Koshare's father," Skunk open his eyes and blinked, "surprises are a daily event. Perhaps the time will come when, during a moment of surprise, I won't even be tempted to spray for I am beginning to see, as this new legend unfolds, that sometimes surprises mark the places where the light grows brighter; where joy replaces fear and where this Skunk, instead of spraying, laughs and laughs and laughs."

"Sku-u-unk, it is getting late," reminded Magpie.

"Oh, yes, of course," mumbled Skunk emerging from his reverie, "now where was I?"

"Skunk, you haven't even started the story yet," scolded Magpie. Can't you see, its almost past Koshare's bedtime?"

"Momma I'm not even sleepy," grumbled Koshare. He sat on the ground leaning against the Thinking Stone. As usual he was chewing on his horn.

"Koshare take that horn out of your mouth and Skunk . . ."

"I know, I know," murmured Skunk wrapping his tail around his feet. "Koshare, when the story's over, promise your mother that'll you'll go straight to bed."

"I promise," said the bored voice.

Magpie fluttered down to Koshare's shoulder and rapped her wing on his nose. "WITHOUT ANY FUSSING!"

"OK, OK."

Skunk's eyelids dropped halfway over his eyes. He cleared his throat and the story began.

"Early one morning," said Skunk watching the last wisps of twilight slip behind the Vanishing Hills, "long before Koshare, the Sun invited all the other stars to go with him on his daily walk across the sky.

All the stars tittered, glimmered and clanked their points together so happy were they to be invited to follow Sun on his journey across the sky.

'Now before we begin our journey,' roared Mighty Sun, 'all you stars must promise me one thing. You must make yourselves invisible all day long so nothing down on earth can see you.'

The Sun was very spoiled after being the only visible star worshiped during the day for billions of years by the inhabitants of Earth.

'If I catch any of you stars twinkling behind my back,' roared Sun, 'I'll abandon you and I'll take away your light.'

Of course, the minute Sun's back was turned the stars glittered, giggled and twinkled behind the Great Sun's back. One star at a time volunteered to stay dull and keep an eye on the

Sun. When the guard star saw the sun turning around it would whisper, "Dimmer, Dimmer," and all the tittering, glittering, stars would fade.

All day long the stars had a wonderful time crossing the blue bowl sky glittering and tittering behind Sun's back. Just before dusk the stars made themselves invisible, and obediently preceded Sun over the edge of earth, falling into place on the darker side of the world. That is, every star except one named Lo Ka Ree.

Lo Ka Ree fell in love with the painted sky. The longer Lo Ka Ree wallowed in the lavenders, golds and crimson hues, the brighter she glimmered. Now just before the Sun slid off the edge of the blue bowl sky, he peered over his shoulder to make sure all the stars were gone. Lo Ka Ree was so much in love that she forgot to fade.

'AH HA!' roared jealous Sun. 'I caught you shining behind my back. You will never leave this place or shine again as long as I'm awake. HA HA HA HO HO HO.'

Just before Sun fell over the edge of the sky, one of his many arms flared out and tossed invisible dust all over La Ka Ree. 'I warned you,' roared the angry Sun. 'I warned you, Lo Ka Ree-e-e-e."

'Look at me,' cried the little star. 'I'm all gone. Nothing can see me. I can't even see myself. Oh, woe is me woe is me.'

Lo Ka Ree wept for two days and three nights. By twilight of the third day, her tears were all used up. But when she opened one eye and looked at herself, lo and behold, she was glittering bright as ever.

"WHOOPEE," shouted Lo Ka Ree, looking at her beloved painted sky. "I am the only glittering star in this whole, beautiful place. LOOK AT ME!"

But the next morning when Sun awakened and climbed into the sky, Lo Ka Ree looked at herself and cried, "Woe is me, Again, I'm nobody. I'm dull all over. Nothing twinkles.

Nothing glitters. Nothing's shining. Oh woe is me.' But at twilight, Lo Ka Ree felt herself glowing hotter, and hotter and hotter. In a matter of seconds, her entire body was bursting with light.

The night Lo Ka Ree called to wisdom-woman-moon. 'Hallo-o-o . . . there, Moon?' she shouted.

After a long pause Moon tilted her deaf ears in the general direction of Lo Ka Ree.

'Somebody call?'

'Yes, yes. It's Lo Ka Ree. Please, I need to speak to you.'

'Go ahead. I can barely hear you, so speak up.'

At the top of her voice Lo Ka Ree shouted, 'Moon, can you explain myself to me? All day long Sun's magic dust keep me invisible. Then, an hour before night, I blaze with light. What is happening to me?''

'How long has this been going on?' replied Old Moon Woman.

'Lets see . . .' shouted Lo Ka Ree. 'I have to think a moment. Perhaps . . . perhaps four nights and five days . . . or is it . . . lets see . . . five days and four nigths? Oh dear . . . Grand-mother Moon, do I have to be absolutely accurate?'

'Not necessarily,' replied Moon. 'A point in time helps me locate the event in my log of universal events. You say the drastic change in your intensity of light started around five days and four nights ago?'

'Yes, something like that,' cracked the voice of Lo Ka Ree who wasn't used to shouting.

'One moment please,' murmured Moon.

The Old Moon Woman thumbed through her log of events. 'This universe,' she mumbled to herself, 'is expanding into such an enormous space and has so many changes occuring every few seconds . . . I wonder . . . how I can possibly keep track of everything? You still there,' she shouted to Lo Ka Ree.

'I'm waiting,' rasped the star, 'but my voice . . . my voice is fading . . . can you still hear me?'

'AH HA!' shrieked Moon. 'At last I have located the occurrence. Lo Ka Ree, are you listening?'

'Tell me, tell me, please,' croaked the voice of La Ka Ree.

'Sun . . .' shouted the Old Moon Woman whose voice grew louder by the second, '. . . is so sleepy by the time he slips off the sky, that he forgets to keep you dull. Therefore, during the twilight hour, just after Sun disappears behind the Vanishing Hills, the painted sky is yours alone. With your dazzling light you lead Earth into and through the darkness of night. Bless you LO-KA-REE.'

'Oh-h-h-h,' rasped Lo Ka Ree, 'now I see. Thank you Moon. Thank you very much.'

'Good night, Lo Ka Ree,' moaned an ancient wind bearing the voice of the wise Old Moon.

''Night, Lo Ka Ree,'' whispered the First Koshare.

Koshare lifted Skunk into his arms and followed Magpie's bobbing tail down the ancient path leading to the cave. Koshare ducked his head and crawled inside. He put Skunk down on his mat of grass and then Koshare curled up next to his father on his own bed.

''Good night, Momma,'' Koshare called to Magpie perched in a bush outside the cave. ''Good night, poppa.''

''Good night, Koshare.''

''Poppa?''

''Yes, Koshare,''

''Remember when all the other stars came out, how hard it was to recognize Lo Ka Ree?''

''Yes.''

''Poppa, Lo Ka Ree sure got a big, BIG family, doesn't she?''

"Big, big family, is right," yawned Skunk. "And do you know something else?"

"What?"

"Just imagine, Koshare, you, me, Magpie . . . everything on earth; the sun and all of our sister/brother planets, all of us belong to the same big, BIG, family as Lo Ka Ree."

"Really?"

"Really."

"Promise?"

"I promise."

BLINK

www.ingramcontent.com/pod-product-compliance
Lightning Source LLC
Chambersburg PA
CBHW020024030726
47499CB00007B/2257